Gabe

7 Brides for 7 Brothers

Ruth Cardello

Don't miss a thing!
www.ruthcardello.com
Sign up for Ruth's Newsletter
forms.aweber.com/form/00/819443400.htm
Join Ruth's Private Fan Group
facebook.com/groups/ruthiesroadies

Also Available

7 Brides for 7 Brothers

Luke – Barbara Freethy (#1)
Gabe – Ruth Cardello (#2)
Hunter – Melody Anne (#3)
Knox – Christie Ridgway (#4)
Max – Lynn Raye Harris (#5)
James – Roxanne St. Claire (#6)
Finn – JoAnn Ross (#7)

Meet the Brannigan brothers—seven sexy brothers who bring the heart and the heat! From bestselling authors Barbara Freethy, Ruth Cardello, Melody Anne, Christie Ridgway, Lynn Raye Harris, Roxanne St. Claire and JoAnn Ross comes a brand-new contemporary romance family series: 7 Brides for 7 Brothers. You won't want to miss a single one!

Gabe – Ruth Cardello

Gabe Brannigan is a Californian real estate mogul who is used to seeing property in terms of dollar signs. When his father dies unexpectedly and leaves him the family ranch, he's annoyed rather than grateful. The conditions of his inheritance include living on the ranch before being able to sell it.

He's ready to walk away from the deal until he meets the sexy, motorcycle-riding ranch caretaker. She's brash and outspoken, rough around the edges. Definitely not his style, but that doesn't stop him from wanting her.

Craving her.

Throwing all caution aside and deciding to have her.

Josephine Ashby has found the perfect place to hide until Mr. Sexy Eyes shows up and announces he is moving in.

A man who doesn't believe in anything, finds himself believing in her.

But will it be enough?

Grab the rest of the series!

Luke – Barbara Freethy
Gabe – Ruth Cardello
Hunter – Melody Anne
Knox – Christie Ridgway
Max – Lynn Raye Harris
James – Roxanne St. Claire
Finn – JoAnn Ross

Dedication

To my friend, Missy. I have always considered myself blessed by the quality of people who wander into my life and steal a piece of my heart. Thank you for your warm welcome and for being so good to my family.

Prologue

Six months earlier.

FEAR IS YOUR opponent's greatest weapon. Give in to it, and you'll lose before the fight begins. Josephine Ashby heard her father's voice in her head and it gave her strength.

She stepped over a toppled lamp in her apartment and scanned the living room. The place wasn't simply ransacked. The damage was vindictive. The cushions on the couch were slashed. The television was smashed. Nothing was taken because what they wanted hadn't been there.

And they were angry.

She stood absolutely still and listened for a sign that anyone was still there. Cautiously, she made her way through each room, picking up a long knife from the kitchen as she went. She couldn't call the police. She had no proof. Not yet.

Back in the living room, Josephine placed the knife down on the arm of a chair and picked up a frame that was face down on the carpet. She touched her father's face through the cracked glass. *I told you we needed to wait before we announced anything, that I needed a little more time to stabilize the power cell. I warned you that accepting money from Raymean would change everything.*

I don't care what the police say. You were not trying to steal the bike. The official cause of Roy Ashby's death was an explosion in his lab at Raymean. His contract was to produce a new power source for the hybrid, silent-running military motorcycle, StealthOff. They *claimed* to have confronted him about the impossibility of his design, which then *supposedly* prompted him to steal the bike to dispose of evidence proving his guilt.

There was no reason for you to do that, no matter what they said to you. And even if you wanted to steal the bike, you wouldn't have ridden it. You knew we were scrapping that version because of its explosive potential. It was a prop, a diversion at your lab, to appease prying eyes while we worked on an alternate fuel source.

She opened the back of the frame and removed her father's photo before dropping the rest to the floor at her feet. The pain of losing him two weeks earlier was still so strong it was numbing. She folded the photo and stuffed it into her back pocket. Even though she'd rented the apartment for five years, a lifetime of following her father around the globe each time he was stationed somewhere new had taught her not to accumulate things or waver when it was time to walk away.

Determined not to lose the fight before it even began, Josephine knew she had to regroup. If she fought them that day, she'd lose. Her father's designs were not unrealistic. They'd just needed more time.

She knew without proof no one would believe her.

Your dream won't die with you, Dad.

I'll finish what we started, clear your name, and whoever is responsible for your death will pay.

Chapter One

GABE BRANNIGAN SWORE when he heard a piece of gravel from the driveway hit the car door of his limited-edition Aston Martin. He would have flown, but a five-hour drive in his new toy had seemed like a good idea. He'd forgotten how rustic his father had kept the ranch.

If Aunt Claire hadn't worn him down with a series of persistent phone calls, he wouldn't have made the trip at all. "You and your brothers practically grew up on that ranch. I can't believe you'd even think of letting it go," she'd said.

"Trust me, it's what Dad wanted," he'd answered without missing a beat. "Otherwise he wouldn't have left it to me with a clause that I live there for a month. That's code for use it as a tax write-off, Gabe."

"You can't do that."

"My accountant assures me I can."

"That's not what I meant and you know it. Your father's ashes were just buried in the canyon next to your mother's. He used to visit her there and I still do."

"I'd gift the whole place to you if I could, but Dad's

will won't allow that. If it's the ashes you're worried about, tell me where they are and I'll have them moved before the property sells."

"Gabriel Colin Brannigan, your mother loved that canyon. That's what matters to me. It should matter to you, too."

"It does," Gabe had said quietly. Not many people would dare speak to Gabe in the tone she'd used, but Aunt Claire marched to her own drummer and wasn't intimidated by anyone. She also reminded Gabe of his mother just enough to hold a special place in his heart. "We should be able to have the new owners agree to allow you access."

"Oh, Gabe, you're missing the point. Your father didn't leave it to me. He wanted you to have it. Have you considered why?"

"Unless there is a buried treasure, and a substantial one, keeping the place isn't worth the month-long occupancy clause. Brannigan Realty just brokered a deal with Wagara and doors are flying open for us. This is what I've been working for. I've moved some of my team from LA to Silicon Valley. We're updating our computer system, headhunting, and reorganizing in preparation for the expansion. I don't have the time or desire to figure out why Dad thought I'd want a forced vacation."

"You are definitely your father's son, but even he knew what was important enough to put work aside for."

"Did he?" Gabe asked curtly, even though he'd admired his father's drive. Colin Brannigan could have lived off the money his parents had left him, but instead he'd used it to create his media empire. Gabe could have taken the easy route, too. He could have tried to springboard off his father's influence in the entertainment world, but like his father, Gabe thrived on the challenge of making his own success. "My father was an amazing man, but he wasn't a nostalgic one. He wouldn't want me visiting his ashes any more than I want to. What do you want me to say, Aunt Claire? I'm not keeping the property. If there is something I can do to make it easier for you to accept that, tell me and I'll add it into the deal. Otherwise, I don't know what else to say."

"Promise me you'll go there before you make your decision."

"I've already decided. It's going to auction."

"Then *undecide* for one weekend. Go down on Friday. Spend the weekend. If on Monday you still want to let it go, I won't say another word."

Not another word? *That* sounded worth a weekend. He could drive down and take work with him. The real estate side of him hated the idea of it selling low because of easy-to-fix cosmetic defects, so there was merit in seeing what state it was in. *Besides, the better the price, the bigger the write-off.*

His optimism dissipated, however, as he drove up the gravel driveway toward the main house. The grounds had not been kept up. The grass stood tall, the paddocks were empty, and the house was in need of painting. Everywhere he looked there were signs of neglect. It certainly wasn't the pristine, multi-million-dollar spread that had once been the envy of their movie-star neighbors. The house itself looked in good condition, but the large inground pool that flanked it was empty and baking in the sun. *I'm not even getting the money from the sale and I'm still disappointed. There's supposedly a full-time caretaker. What the hell is he taking care of?*

Gabe parked and was about to head into the house when he heard music. He followed the sound to the driveway of one of the guest houses. His eyebrows rose in appreciation at the expanse of long, bronzed legs that led to the perfectly rounded ass of a woman in cutoff jean shorts who was bent over the open hood of an old sedan. Although his taste in women was normally more sophisticated, some asses were universally attractive no matter how one dressed them.

Whatever she was working on, her focus was so intent she didn't notice his approach. He knew he should say something, but he gave himself a moment to enjoy the view. Could any man have resisted?

The little part of his brain that was capable of thought at that moment wondered who she was. The car she was working on was an older, inexpensive model. She might be the caretaker's daughter. He cleared his throat at that thought and hoped to hell she was well over eighteen.

At the sound she spun around with a wrench held high in one hand. Her gaze raked over him, narrowing with displeasure. It was a response he wasn't used to in a woman. "This is private property," she said in a firm voice, still holding the wrench as if she might crack him in the head with it if he stepped closer.

"Is it?" All better retorts were lost as he took in her full, glistening beauty. She looked like she was in her mid-twenties. Long brown hair was swept up in a loose ponytail, allowing dark tendrils to fall and frame her face. One of her arms was tattooed with the face of a dragon, which normally would have been a turnoff, but he was intrigued by it. Dark brown eyes glared at him, while her chest heaved up and down beneath a thin, white tank top and bra that did nothing to conceal her response to his perusal. A half smile curled his lips. He was old enough to know that sexual chemistry didn't require context nor did it always respect personal preferences. Sometimes it was simply there and this time it was—stronger than he remembered feeling with anyone for a very long time. The five-hour drive might not have been a waste of time after all.

"Yes, so you can't be here. Leave your name, though, and I'll tell the owners you came by."

Who the hell is this beauty? "I'd rather have *your* name."

Her raised arm shook. "Mine?"

Her stall increased his curiosity, and he stepped closer. He lowered his voice. "Yes, yours."

She glanced quickly to the left then the right and swore. "Listen, I don't want to hurt you, but you need to leave."

"I'm not going anywhere." He inched closer, and his breathing deepened like a hunter sensing his prey was about to bolt. He was mid-step when she struck, and with a swift move he recognized from his kick-boxing days, she hooked his ankle with hers and pulled his foot out from beneath him. He fell forward, but righted himself before he hit the ground.

She used the advantage of surprise to race out of his reach. He turned in time to see her retrieve a 9mm Beretta from her toolbox. In a stance proving she was no novice, she pointed the gun directly at him. "Yes, you are. I don't want to shoot you, but I will if I have to." She clicked the safety off.

Her eyes glittered, her dark hair blew in the wind behind her, and she went from a ten on his hotness scale to an unbelievable fifteen. *Damn.* He'd never been into bondage or thought giving control over to a woman could be sexy, but he was willing to experiment with it for a taste of her. He kept that thought to himself because she didn't look like she was thinking the same. He referenced his suit and Stefano Bemer loafers. "Easy, tiger. Do I look like someone you need to run off with a gun?"

She assessed him over from head to toe again. "Yes."

Okay, not what I expected. It might be time to tell her my name. "I'm Gabe Brannigan, the owner of this property."

She frowned. "Colin Brannigan owns the ranch."

"My father passed away a few weeks ago."

She lowered the gun and her expression softened for the first time. "I'm sorry to hear that."

He sensed her calming. It was strange to be so attuned to a woman without even knowing her name. "I drove down to look the place over before it goes up for auction."

"Auction? You're selling it?" Her face paled.

"Yes." Her level of distress at the idea was disconcerting. He warned himself not to get involved. Disappointing as it was, the longer he had to think about it, the more he knew he had to take the possibility of bedding her off the table. Also, having her on any table. *No, having her at all.* It wasn't the gun that concerned him. Plenty of people owned them, and a woman alone on a ranch was smart to protect herself. It was the desperation he'd seen in her eyes that was a warning bell. She was too wild for his taste and potentially too needy. "Where is Frank Muller?"

She swallowed visibly. "His daughter in New Mexico had a baby. Two months premature. He went out there to help her until she's settled."

"And left you in charge?"

She looked away evasively. "Yes."

"How long has he been gone?"

"A few months, but he'll be back soon."

"He can take his time. I'm not impressed with how he kept the place up. I'll have my renovation crew here on Monday." There was no way a home, especially one that had once been a Brannigan residence, would be sold in this condition. His name was associated with luxury. His reputation was for finding the very best for those who could afford it. Even if it was a losing deal, he intended to bring the house up to its previous glory before it opened to the public. His competition would love to fill social media with unflattering images of a project he was associated with.

"No," she burst out. "Don't do that."

He arched an eyebrow.

She swore again. "I mean it's not necessary. If you give me a couple weeks I can have everything spit polished and ready for you to show."

"I don't have a couple weeks." Her face tightened as he spoke. There it was, the desperation that made him wonder if she'd point the gun at him again. "Plus, there's more work than you could do alone."

"It'll be done. I give you my word," she said with Girl Scout seriousness that brought a smile to his lips. In his world nothing could be counted on that wasn't written into a contract. Nothing. Everything happened in writing—even his father's final wishes.

"I'll make you a deal."

She watched him warily and waited.

He held out his hand. "First, give me the gun."

She hesitated, clicked the safety back on, emptied the bullets into her pocket, then handed it to him.

He replaced the gun in her toolbox then returned to face her. "My crew will be here on Monday, but I'll consider letting you continue to stay here while I have it worked on if . . ." she took a deep breath, holding his eyes with quiet strength, ". . . you tell me your name." Regardless of her rough edges, he'd never seen a more beautiful woman. She effortlessly inspired a thousand illicit thoughts he kept to himself.

JOSEPHINE DIDN'T LIKE lying, but she could do it with a straight poker face if she had to. Some lies were necessary; they protected or removed obstacles in a way the truth never would. She'd come up with her first alias when she was seventeen and her father had been shot during a deployment in the Middle East. Having always been a tinkerer on the side, her father had been working on a fabric cheaper than the Army-issued bulletproof gear. According to her father, she had a "scientifically inclined brain," so she'd understood the roadblock he'd hit in his design. Bored in a regular classroom, she'd excelled in online courses that allowed her to dig into how things worked. She'd tested out of high school at sixteen, but even the online college classes hadn't held her interest. Her father's work had. Her mother had left when Josephine was an infant; she'd never seen the point in searching for her. *Why bother?*

Her father had been her parent and her hero.

He was creative with his inventions, but would hit a ceiling where his dream exceeded his ability. With a little help, she'd known he could sell one of his ideas for enough money that he could retire. So, Josephine had gone online and pretended to be a professor from a foreign university. She'd contacted and opened dialogue with key people in a variety of fields who were experimenting with the various polymers. The more she learned, the more she shared, and in return, the more they shared with her.

At first she'd been intimidated by their degrees and titles, but as more and more of her ideas were well received and implemented, she became more confident and sought after. Over the last eleven years she'd used three different online aliases to build a dark web network of scientists from a wide range of fields who collaborated anonymously on each other's projects. Their help enabled her father to eventually finish his bulletproof fabric design, which he sold to the Army for a modest amount and bought a home in Connecticut. Over the years, her covert think tank had gelled into a community where great minds brought their questions and received feedback from peers with different yet equally qualified viewpoints. No questions asked. No credit awarded. All participation guaranteed reciprocal support from the community. Their common goal: saving lives and moving humanity forward, everything from reducing the production cost of portable water purification systems for third world countries to improving the shields for the international space station.

Lying for a good cause wasn't lying at all—not in her book.

That philosophy allowed her to look Gabe directly in

the eye and create a new identity on the spot. "Josie Arlington."

His smile was confident, smooth, and sexy as hell. "That wasn't so hard, was it?"

"Not at all," she said, hating how her own lips betrayed her and curled in an answering smile. Her heart was beating wildly but not due to who she'd feared he was when he first arrived or that he'd drastically reduced her timeline for finishing the new fuel cell for StealthOff. Both occurrences should have been more important than how the distribution of melanin in his irises scattered and reflected the light resulting in a complex, almost artistic blend of blue, green, and brown. She knew the hues created were dictated by how her own eyes perceived the variation in light rather than actually being that color, but that knowledge didn't make them any less striking.

She tried to dismiss her attraction to him. People were predisposed to react to a certain combination of pheromones and physical symmetry. Also, biologically, she was likely at a stage in her menstrual cycle where she would naturally find herself drawn to healthy, muscular males. Hell, it was also exciting to meet a man she couldn't knock down or run off.

Had that ever happened before?

She realized she was standing there, smiling at him—in adoration—and gave herself an inner shake. *Stop. This is not the time to think about how long it's been since I've had sex. Tim was a year ago—no, two. Shit, no wonder I can't think straight.*

But I have to.

His presence alone is enough to risk everything I've worked for.

No one can or will know who I am or what I'm doing. I'm so close. Once again, all I need is a little more time. I will clear Dad's name.

That's what matters, not this man or the flutters I get when he looks at me.

Think. His father left him the place, and he wants to sell it. How can I use that to buy myself more time? Do I need to go from someone who just tried to send him face first into the dirt to someone else? She'd spent most of her life either online, in a lab working on something with her father, or exercising, the latter because her father had always maintained that a good brain required a healthy body. Half her childhood had been her father's version of boot camp. She could spar with the best in a variety of martial arts, but flirt? That was one skill she hadn't acquired over her mostly solitary life, but she decided to give it her best shot. "You won't even notice I'm here. I've been using this guest house, but I can move to wherever is most convenient for you." She awkwardly fluttered her eyelashes at him.

"You're welcome to stay where you are for now."

"Thank you." Her attempt at a purr resulted in a cough. He was watching her so closely she started to sweat nervously. She raised a hand to wipe her forehead and noticed how his eyes fell to her breasts.

This might be easier than I thought.

She ran a hand across her collarbone slowly, trying to make the move look nonchalant. It might have been wishful thinking, but she could have sworn his cheeks flushed slightly. "I'm surprised you want to sell the place so quickly."

His eyes returned to hers, and the hunger she saw there sent warmth flooding through her and temporarily muddled her thoughts. Desire wasn't foreign to her. She wasn't a virgin. She'd had sex with two and a half men. The car mechanic had been great in bed, but had also wanted to bed everyone she knew. The physicist had been faithful, but he couldn't bring her to climax and his rationalizations for why were tedious. Then there'd been Tim, a web designer she'd met in a coffee shop. He'd seemed promising. Smart. Funny. Good kisser. In the end, though, he'd been unable to sustain an erection. If there'd been any penetration at all, it had been halfway, so Josephine didn't give him full credit.

None of them had sent flames licking through her with just a look. She ran her tongue over her bottom lip, imagining how he'd taste. "It's beautiful." *He's beautiful.*

His eyes dilated and he took a deep breath. "It is, but it would never fit my lifestyle."

"Are you sure? You haven't been here in a while. There's no need to rush into a decision." Her husky tone surprised even herself. She was trying to convince him to put off the sale of the ranch, not hop into bed with her.

Keyword: not. *No matter how deliciously fit he proba-bly is beneath that suit.* She took a moment to appreciate the width of his shoulders and the strong cut of his jaw. It was insanely easy to imagine loosening his tie then using it to pull his face down to hers.

God, I've obviously spent too much time alone lately.

He leaned closer. "That's why I'm here until Sunday. My aunt thinks it'll change my mind." His face hovered just above hers. "It won't. Once I make a decision I don't second-guess it." His breath tickled her parted lips. "Usually."

Chapter Two

GABE HADN'T GROWN one real estate deal into a brand with instant name recognition, as well as exponentially increasing profit each year, by chance. His friends called it dogged determination. His competition said he was obsessed with winning. Either way, Gabe was used to getting what he wanted, but he wasn't used to wanting anyone or anything so clearly wrong for him.

He could only imagine how he'd look back at that weekend. *What did Luke do when Dad died? He reunited with a woman he claims is the love of his life. What did I do? I screwed a gun-toting ninja who said she was supposed to be at the ranch but was really just a squatter.*

Good?

It was amazing.

The right thing to do?

Hell no, but I'd do it again.

Up close, Josie was even more tempting. Instead of the store-bought perfumes that sometimes assaulted his senses, Josie was deliciously natural. He breathed in the scent of her and savored the heat that seared through him. *One taste of those sweet lips. That's all I need.*

Their eyes met and Gabe was momentarily enthralled by the complexity of his attraction to her. It went deeper than the perfection of her ass and the lush fullness of her lips. She was a fascinating mix of awkward and fierce. How much of that would carry over into the bedroom? If she'd looked a hair less vulnerable in that moment, he might have thrown caution to the wind and carried her into the guest house to find out. He couldn't, though, not when she looked up at him with just enough innocent yearning to confuse him.

Something about her was bringing out a protective side of him he would have sworn he didn't have. "Do you have any place to go when you leave here?"

She chewed her bottom lip. "I'll figure it out. I always do."

He needed more. More answers. More of her. "How do you know Frank?"

Her eyes darkened. "He was a friend of my father."

"Was?"

"My father died six months ago," she said just above a whisper.

So, she lost her father recently as well. A sad thing to have in common. It stirred feelings he'd been hoping to avoid. His father wouldn't want to be missed. He'd want his children to continue to forge ahead. "Were you close?"

"Inseparable. I miss him so much it's hard to feel anything else. How about you?"

"I didn't know my father was sick. I hadn't seen him

for a while. We were both too busy." It wasn't something Gabe had thought much about until just then. He'd admired his father. Respected him. But missed him? That would have required them spending time together. *When did I last see him or Skype with him?* The close Irish family he'd been born into, the one with seven brothers who all cared about each other and had parents who spent vacations with them had disappeared when his mother died. Nannies and excuses were the norm in the void Kathleen Brannigan had left in her wake. Twenty-three years was a long time to miss anyone, but he remembered everything about her. How his father laughed louder whenever she was around. How she'd made everything special from a walk through the woods to a cup of hot chocolate on a cold evening. For some inexplicable reason, a memory of her tending to a scrape on his knee came back with painful vividness. Her death had shaken and nearly destroyed his world. He wouldn't let his father's death reopen that old wound. *But how was it I didn't feel the same loss when I heard about my father?*

He rubbed a hand over his forehead. The direction of the conversation was giving him a headache. "How long have you been here?"

"Since I lost my father. Frank said I could stay with him until I sorted some things out."

"What kind of things?"

She looked as uncomfortable with his questions as he'd felt with hers. "I needed some time to think."

It wasn't the whole truth. She was holding something

back, but he had no idea where to begin to guess what. "Did you leave a job behind?"

She took a step back. "If you don't mind, I really should finish changing the spark plugs in the Ford."

Gabe would have offered to help, but his knowledge of what happened beneath the hood of a car was limited to articles in men's magazines. "I could have it towed to a local garage."

She shook her head vehemently. "I'm almost finished anyway. If you'd arrived fifteen minutes later I would have been gone." She shrugged one shoulder apologetically. "I was heading to town for groceries when I realized why the battery was dead again. You won't find much in the main house, but after I finish, I can pick up supplies for you, too."

He nodded toward his vehicle. "Or we could take my car into town."

She looked past him and her eyes widened with recognition. "Is that an Aston Martin 2016 Vanquish Zagato Coupe?"

His chest puffed with pride. "It is."

Gabe was quickly forgotten as she strode toward his car. He kept pace with her, completely understanding the look of wonder on her face. He'd felt the same the first time he'd seen it.

She ran her hand reverently over the wing mirrors. "I didn't think it was out yet."

"A small number became available early. This one was a gift from a grateful client."

"Nice gift," she said in a husky tone he suddenly wanted to hear her say his name in, but all of her attention was on the car. "Upgraded 6.0L V12 power-train. Zero to sixty in three-point-five seconds. Herringbone carbon-fiber body. Quad exhaust. Their suspension is perfection. Whenever Aston Martin and Zagato collaborate they make more than a car—they make art. Look at the wheel arch and how it blends into the Zagato rear view. Every line is nothing short of breathtaking." She frowned as she came across what he'd suspected he'd done to the car earlier. "Is that a scratch?"

Amusement at her reaction replaced his earlier aggravation. He shrugged. "Gravel driveway."

She ran a hand lightly over the imperfection. "These babies are hand-painted, but that's actually a good thing. I have a polishing machine that can take the mark right out. A little cleaner fluid, then some wax, and it would be good as new. Better, if you trust me to coat it with a sealant that will prevent this from happening again."

"Thanks, but I have a service who does that sort of thing." No way was she working on this car. Sex with a woman he barely knew? Completely feasible. Letting anyone who hadn't been vetted attempt to buff out a scratch on his Aston Marin? That was crazy talk.

"Of course," she said, letting her hand drop from the car. "Well, I should get back to my car."

"Have dinner with me tonight."

Her eyes flew to his and he saw desire flash in them before she looked away. "My fridge is pretty empty, and

I'm sure the main house is worse."

"There must be restaurants nearby. Which one is your favorite?"

"I always eat here."

"Always?"

"Yes." She hugged her arms across her stomach. "I don't like to go out."

Another warning bell went off in his head. Was she hiding from someone? The law? She obviously knew her way around cars. Who was she? Her eyes met his and the questions fell away. His heart began to thud wildly in his chest. "We'll have something delivered then." He held his breath as he waited for her answer.

Indecision darkened her beautiful eyes and made him want her even more. Not since middle school had he issued an invitation and been uncertain as to what the response would be.

"Okay," she said. "At the main or the guest house?"

A slow, satisfied smile spread across his face. "The main house." He checked his watch. "At six o'clock. That will give me time to shower, order food, and get some calls in while you finish working on your car."

"Six o'clock." She looked adorably uncertain. "Should I bring anything?"

"No, I'll have everything ready." *Food. Wine. Condoms.*

The way she blushed made him wonder if he'd uttered his list out loud. When she didn't address it, he decided her mind had merely gone where his had. She took a step back and said, "I'm sorry. I appreciate the offer but . . ."

He closed the distance between them, stopping just before touching her. "What are you afraid of?"

She looked torn for a moment, then she raised her chin. "Nothing. I simply don't want you to think—"

"You don't want me to imagine how incredible it would be to kiss you until you were saying my name over and over? Begging for more? Too late, it's already damn near all I can think about."

Her sweet lips rounded in a surprised circle. "We just met."

"I'm willing to overlook that."

She blinked a few times quickly. "Wow, that's quite an ego you have there."

He raised a hand to the side of her face and caressed it gently. "Want to humble me? Have dinner with me and prove how resistible I actually am."

"That would be easy because you're not my type at all. In fact, you're the opposite of my type."

"Then dinner should be no problem." He walked over to the driver's side of his car, opened the door and retrieved his laptop bag. "See you at six." He shot her his sexiest smile and loved how her cheeks flushed before she turned away.

Once inside the main house, the first call he made was to the security firm he used for background checks on everyone he dealt with. Part of his success in real estate was due to how he checked for potential risks. He left nothing to chance. Others might be confused by a deal that fell through unexpectedly, but that was because they didn't do their homework. Mining personal data was the newest gold rush. Everything worth knowing about a person could discretely be bought for the right price. He gave them Josie's name, physical description, and her relationship to Frank Muller. It wasn't much, but he'd provided them with less in the past and been impressed.

I'll know her history before dinner.
And every inch of her before morning.

JOSEPHINE LOOKED THROUGH her closet a second time before giving in to the humor of the moment. When she'd fled the East Coast she thought she'd planned for everything. She'd taken what she could carry on her bike and stored the rest of her tools and technology with a local man she knew through her father. Over time, she'd had her things shipped to her and purchased what she needed online. Hair dye, colored contacts, fake tattoos, computer servers. Slowly she'd crafted not only a new identity for herself off the grid, but she also built a hidden lab where she could continue to develop the alternate powercell for the bike.

StealthOff could run loudly on a large number of combustibles. The hybrid engine worked on everything from olive oil to jet fuel because it was designed to function in the most challenging situations. Constructed from metal alloys virtually indestructible, it had airless tires that most bullets couldn't penetrate. It could be dropped from a plane, submerged in water, or driven briefly through fire and still function. Her father had watched too many Bond movies, but that was his magic. Nothing was impossible. In the very worst of imagined scenarios, additional wheels dropped down, steadying the bike, and a person could be strapped on. It could then be driven remotely by an encrypted transmission which would allow for extraction of an injured soldier. What it couldn't do yet was not explode when the secondary power source, the one that allowed it to run silently, was engaged for more than five minutes. All previous attempts to keep the lithium-ion batteries cool either failed or required cumbersome systems that would be impractical to maintain in a hostile environment. Others in the field were experimenting with lithium-air as an alternative, but Josephine was branching out to magnesium-ion and sodium-ion because of their potential for better energy density and overall lower cost. *Now if I could just stabilize the discharge.*

That, however, wasn't the most immediate problem.

How could I have everything I need for the lab and not have a single dress? Not one.

In practical white panties and a matching white bra, she studied her reflection in the full-length mirror on the back of the door. *In some alternate universe I could be sexy.* She let herself imagine his expression if she went to dinner in full makeup, with her hair smooth and cascading over her bare shoulders in a backless black dress. She ran her hand up the outside of her thigh and could almost feel his touch.

She shook her head at the passion she saw in her eyes. *Never going to happen. It's not worth the risk.* One slip, one action that brought attention to herself, and she could ruin everything. *The goal of dinner is to convince him that he shouldn't give me another thought. He needs to leave on Sunday thinking there's no rush to return.*

I need a window of time to pack up my lab.

And a moving truck.

If all goes well, his crew will arrive late on Monday, and I'll be long gone. To where, I don't know, but I can't stay here.

The fake wall she'd erected to conceal her lab in the back of the six-car garage would fool most people, but not a renovation team with building specs.

And not a man who once lived here.

I need to keep him occupied, distracted long enough that he won't look around. She lifted a T-shirt off a hanger and grabbed a pair of jeans. *But not so occupied that he wants to stay. So, maybe this is perfect.* A moment later she brushed out her shoulder-length hair and made a face at how it seemed to have a mind of its own. Rather than tame and sophisticated, it preferred wild and unmanageable. She threw it back in a ponytail again and inspected her face one last time. *As far as primping goes, brushing my teeth will have to suffice.*

Does it really matter what he thinks of me? Am I seriously worried what Mr. Sexy Smile will think of my near-

invisible eyelashes?

That's my new priority?

She squared her shoulders. *Only because my plan to distract him relies on him remaining at least a little attracted to me.*

Not because all he has to do is look at me and I'm a quivering mass of sexual frustration.

She sighed and turned away from her reflection. The hardest lie to maintain was one uttered to someone who knew the truth.

Chapter Three

GABE HAD JUST paid the private chef he'd hired for the evening and was in the process of walking him to the door when his phone rang. He shut the door behind the departing chef and groaned when he saw the name of the caller.

Luke.

He normally enjoyed hearing from his younger brother. Luke's stories were never dull. Whether it was a detailed retelling of nearly dying while hanging off the side of a mountain or a colorful description of what goes through a person's head when his parachute deploys late, Luke was entertaining. If Gabe had to guess, though, they weren't about to have one of those phone calls.

"Luke," Gabe reluctantly answered while walking back into the dining room to light the candles. No, they weren't necessary, but like an expensive suit, lighting made an impression and sent a message. He and Josie were engaged in a game of sorts, and this was his move. Where the evening would lead, well, that would be her move.

"Gabe, did you make it down to the ranch?"

So not in the mood for this. "I did. I'm here until Sunday."

"Does it look the same?"

"Yes and no." Luke clearly misunderstood Gabe's purpose for being there. "I haven't changed my mind about letting it go to auction. Before you start listing reasons why you think I should reconsider or jump into some reverie of how Mom taught us to ride quads here—"

"Did she? I don't remember."

The hint of regret in Luke's voice stopped Gabe short. For someone who had often put himself in danger for the thrill of it, Luke had a softer side that Gabe made an effort not to trample. Gabe didn't see his mother in himself, but he saw her in Luke. Just glimpses. That side of him made it easy to imagine Luke married with children. He cared about things on a deeper level than Gabe did.

Gabe was more like his father and not the best of who he'd been, at least according to Hunter, his fraternal twin. He'd rather be at work than anywhere else. He was competitive by nature and felt most alive when striking a deal. Although he loved his family, they came second to his ambition. If he couldn't buy and sell it for a profit, chances were he had little interest in it. At the end of the day, money and power were all that endured. His father had taught him that. Still, that didn't mean Gabe needed to be an ass every moment of every day.

"I found some photo albums in Dad's old office. Do you want them?"

"Not the scrapbooking brother, Gabe," Luke said dryly.

Gabe laughed. "Who is? Maybe Aunt Claire will take them and make digital copies of the photos."

"Good idea."

"How are things going at the resort? I still can't believe you're keeping the place. What happened to my brother the adventurer?"

"I found a new adventure. And I'm happy. Lizzie and Kaitlyn have changed the way I look at life. I know you're set on walking away from the ranch, but don't rush. Lizzie gave me that advice when I considered selling the resort. Dad had something he wanted each of us to know about him and ourselves. Somehow he knew I belonged with Lizzie, and he brought us back together. There's something at that ranch he wanted you to discover for yourself."

"You lucked out with a simple deed transfer. The ranch came with a one-month occupancy clause. One full month. Even if I wanted to keep it, I don't have time for that."

"You sound just like Dad." *And I know that isn't a compliment.*

"I love you, Luke, but I'm not having this conversation."

"He never had time to talk either. I wonder if that was what he regretted in the end. Maybe your inheritance isn't so much about the ranch as it is a reminder that some things are worth putting aside time for."

Luke's comment cut uncomfortably close, so Gabe brushed it off. "Or he knew it had fallen into disrepair and left it to someone who wouldn't let memories blind him to the fact that none of us need this place anymore. When was the last time you were here? The last time any of us were? It's a relic from our childhood, like an old box of Legos stored in an attic. The time has come to let it go."

The doorbell rang, hopefully announcing Josie's arrival. "Speaking of going, my company just arrived. It was good to hear from you, though, and I'm happy for you. I really am. Tell Lizzie I'm glad she's back."

"I will—"

Gabe hung up before Luke had time to say any more. He forced himself to walk instead of race to the door, a fact that brought a smile to his lips. He couldn't remember the last time he was so into a woman that everything else fell away. He hadn't gotten through more than a couple emails because his thoughts kept going back to her. There wasn't a deal proposal that rivaled the exceptional memory of how she'd tried to knock him off his feet. More than once he'd closed his eyes and remembered how she'd looked standing there, gun in hand, chest heaving, looking like Daisy Duke's biker sister. In other words—hotter than hell.

That's all it took to shoot his concentration to hell.

He didn't want or need to know everything about her, so he wasn't disappointed that she'd arrived before the background check on her had. Being with her rivaled how he felt when he closed a deal. Like an adrenaline junkie who wants to hop right back on a rollercoaster as soon as it ends, Josie was a ride Gabe wasn't in a hurry to end.

The uncertain look on Josie's face when he opened the door sent him on an internal tail spin. She was a confusing mixture of bold and vulnerable, which fueled conflicting desires within him. Part of him wanted to pull her into his arms and kiss her until the fire he'd seen earlier was back in her eyes. Another part of him wanted to reassure her that regardless of how he felt, not a single thing would happen between them unless she wanted it just as much. He settled for opening the door wider and saying, "Come in."

She looked him over but didn't move to enter the house. "You changed into another suit."

He straightened his already perfectly placed tie. "I did."

She glanced down at her own attire then around the foyer. "Is anyone else here?"

A smile curled his lips. "No."

"Oh, okay." She stepped past him and tucked her hands into the front pockets of her jeans. "I didn't change my mind about not wanting to go anywhere."

He closed the door and moved to stand next to her. "Good, because I had a meal prepared for us here." He placed a hand on her lower back and was surprised at how tense she was. He studied her profile and asked himself if he could have misread her response to him earlier. She wasn't looking like a woman who wanted to be swept up into his bedroom. She seemed nervous but determined.

She rubbed her hands up and down her arms as if trying to warm up. "Was that who was here earlier? I thought we were having something delivered."

"I prefer healthy when I can. I eat a lot of chicken and—"

"Me, too," she said and smiled for the first time. "Free range and hormone free. I tried to be a vegetarian once, but there are some meats I couldn't give up. Do you like fish? I don't, but I love—"

"Salmon?"

She nodded. "Yes."

"I could eat it twice a week and not get sick of it, but it has to be perfectly prepared. I'm glad you like it because it's what we're having tonight. I found a local chef who is known for his salmon dish. I've never used him before, but we'll find out together if he's the culinary genius he claims to be."

She relaxed slightly beneath his hand. "He really said that?"

"Right after I asked him not to overcook the fish."

"You didn't." She smiled again.

He shrugged and led her toward the dining room. "I know what I want; why settle for less?"

Her smile faded. "Most people don't think that way. We're all working on surviving."

The seriousness of her tone made him stop and turn

to look down at her. He bit back the first several responses that came to him. He wanted to say that she didn't have to live that way, that he'd help her. He wanted to ask her if someone had hurt her then hunt the bastard down. He had a feeling, though, that once he opened that door it would be a rabbit hole to trouble. He didn't know her. Did he want to? Not just her body . . .

Was it possible to know one without the other? He'd planned the evening thinking it was, but suddenly he wasn't so sure. Brannigan Realty was gearing up for expansion. He needed his head in the game.

Advice his father had once given him echoed in his head. "If you're looking for a reason to fail, Gabe, you'll find one. There will always be an excuse to not finish something. The people who succeed are the ones who stay focused and get things done."

It was difficult to imagine his father falling for the free spirt his mother had been. Gabe realized that he thought of his father only in terms of who he'd become after his mother had died. Being on the ranch *was* bringing back memories. There'd been another side of him. Before the nannies. Before he spent more time at the office than he spent at home. Flashes of his father, sitting at the dinner table, his robust laugh booming in response to something his mother had said. That man would have asked Josie if someone had hurt her, and he would have made it right.

Which man am I?

"Are you okay?" Josie asked and frowned when he

laughed without humor at the irony of her question.

He didn't feel okay at all. His stomach was twisted in a painful knot. He wasn't normally introspective, but his emotions were heightened. More than anything he wished he could call his father and ask him if it had been worth it. If Colin Brannigan had a second chance at life, would he have chosen to love the woman he was fated to lose too soon?

Would he still have had seven sons if he knew he'd become a man none of them knew how to reach?

And what would he say about Josie? Would he tell Gabe to run, not walk, away or pull her into the shelter of his arms?

I never called Dad for advice. I always knew what I wanted. What is wrong with me?

He thought back to what Luke had said, "You may not think you're grieving for Dad, but you are." *Is that what this is? I'm grieving?*

Josie's probably fine.

I'm the one with problems.

He realized he hadn't answered her yet and forced a smile. "Sorry, I'm a grouch when I'm hungry."

She studied his expression, then a cautious smile returned to her face. "That's something else we have in common."

His hand tensed on her back. She was beginning to trust him and he suddenly regretted putting out the candles. Yes, he wanted a night with her, but he also wanted to know what had put those shadows beneath her eyes.

➦ Would one cost him the other?

And, if so, which did he want more?

JOSEPHINE WAS A wreck by the time she sat in the chair Gabe held out for her. She'd expected to be passing each other slices of pizza from cardboard boxes. She hadn't expected a romantic setting, her favorite meal, and for him to look even better than he had earlier.

He left the room for a moment, and she slumped in her seat. *Am I a fool to think I can control this situation?*

Or him.

I should have had a plan B. Something with chloroform.

No, unlike in the movies, it actually takes five to seven minutes for a person to pass out from it.

Tranquilizers? Even if I had them, I'd feel guilty about leaving anyone in that state.

She sat up straight. *Toughen up, Josephine. You can do this. Just keep him occupied without sleeping with him. Unless he comes out of that kitchen in nothing but an apron.* A flash fantasy of him doing just that brought a wistful smile to her face. Did he look as good out of the suit as he did in it? She closed her eyes and let herself imagine his muscles flexing as he walked toward her. With one strong sweep, he'd clear the table and haul her to him. His kiss would be—

"Josie?"

Her eyes flew open at his amused tone, and she

blushed clear to her toes. He was standing beside the table, fully dressed, with two plates of salmon and vegetables. She swallowed hard and said the first excuse that came to mind. "Just saying grace." *Oh, shit, I shouldn't have said that. There are lies and then there are instant tickets to hell. Throwing God under the bus as a cover for lusty daydreams can't be good.*

He gave her a long look then placed her plate in front of her. "My family is Irish. We used to say grace when we were children. My mother insisted on it."

God, if you're listening, I'll start saying grace. I promise. "That sounds like a nice way to grow up."

"It was. I don't know that my mother was all that religious, but she wanted us to remember to be grateful." Gabe placed his food down and took his seat across from her.

"What happened to her?"

"She died when I was ten." He made a face. "Until I came here I hadn't realized how different things were when she was part of our lives." He stopped and nodded at her food. "Eat. I don't know why I'm talking about this. She's been gone a long time."

Josephine understood why. Losing her father had been like losing a piece of herself, a part she wasn't sure how to go on without. She reached out for his hand, but closed her hand around one of the napkins instead. She had to remind herself that she barely knew him. "She sounds like a beautiful woman."

He smiled sadly. "She was. Sometimes I wonder who

my brothers and I would be today had she lived."

Although she was painfully awkward at flirting, this wasn't awkward at all because she cared more about making him feel better than how she sounded. "Your brothers? How many do you have?"

"Six."

"Holy shit," she said then stopped when she realized her exclamation sounded even more vulgar in the sophistication of the setting. Having been raised by her father and his Army buddies, she could swear right along with them. She'd tried to tone it down as she got older, but it still came out now and then. She also didn't want him to think she was passing judgment on the size of his family. "Sorry."

He chuckled. "Don't apologize. Most people probably think exactly the same when they hear there are so many of us. Dad used to joke it was because Mom was determined to have a girl. She might have kept going if my brothers hadn't been so wild."

Relaxing, Josephine took a bite of the most delicious salmon she'd ever tasted and chewed it before asking, "All wild except you?"

"I was the serious one." He opened a bottle of wine and offered to fill her glass.

She nodded and said, "Tell me about them."

Humor lit his eyes. "James is the oldest. Everything he touches turns to gold. When we were kids he was the first up any new hill. Hunter is my age. He was born with the gift of being able to talk me into almost anything. And it usually turned out badly for me."

"Is he your twin?"

"Fraternal. I'm three minutes older."

"Who is next?"

"Max. He would throw himself in front of a bear if one were coming for any of us. When he became a Navy SEAL, it wasn't much of a surprise. Then Luke. He's wild like Hunter, but the two don't see the similarities. And Knox. He's the comedian of our family. At least, he was. He took Dad's death hard. And finally poor Finn. Mom really wanted a girl. That's probably all he remembers about her. He was very young when she died. How about you? Do you have any brothers or sisters?"

"No, it was always just me and Dad." Her throat closed as emotion welled up, and she blinked quickly. Loss was something her father had understood well, but when he'd spoken of a fallen Army buddy he never did so in terms of his pain. Instead, he always listed their acts of valor and highlighted the best of who they'd been. Holding to that tradition, she said, "He was a good man. A proud American, but one who could appreciate patriotism in people from other countries. He was a humble combination of dreamer and soldier. He would have given every one of his designs away if I hadn't convinced him that we also needed to put food on the table. To him, the big picture was always the most important one and there was always hope. I liked the world a whole lot better when I saw it through his eyes."

Gabe took her hand in his and gave it a squeeze. "Is

that why you're hiding on my ranch?"

"I'm not hiding." She snatched her hand away and gulped down half the wine in her glass. *Calm down. He doesn't know anything. He's simply asking questions the way I did.*

"You are." He sat back and took a sip of his wine before answering. "You yourself said you won't leave the ranch to go to dinner. When was the last time you went out with friends? Or on a date?"

When Josephine went to put her fork down, she accidentally sent it flying across the table. He caught it calmly as it was coming to a skidding halt in front of him. She asked, "When was the last time *you* did?"

"Last night." He held it out to her with a cocky smile.

Last night? I bet she was beautiful, perfect. Probably a model. Or some rich man's daughter. Not the type to send utensils flying around the room.

It doesn't matter.

After he leaves on Sunday, I won't see him again.

"Curious as to which it was? Friends or a date?" he asked.

"Not at all."

His smile widened. "It was a work dinner, actually. So colleagues rather than friends."

She let out the breath she'd been holding but met his eyes boldly. "I really couldn't care less."

He placed her fork next to her plate, but her declaration seemed to amuse him. "My ego is taking a beating with you. Just so you know, I don't want to picture you with anyone else. As long as you're not married to him, I don't actually need to know."

Her eyes flew to his. "If there *was* someone I wouldn't be here with you. I'm not that kind of person."

There it was, that cocky smile of his. "So, there's no one. Good."

A splash of irritation was followed by grudging admiration of his interrogation skills. *I need to be more careful. I've already shared too much.* As Gabe topped off her wine she realized what was loosening her tongue. She pushed the glass to the side and stood. "Thank you for dinner. It was wonderful."

He rose to his feet. "Did I mention I'm Irish?"

"You did."

"In Ireland it's customary to thank the person who provided dinner."

"I said thank you."

He stepped closer. "It's usually done with a kiss."

She held her ground, both because she retreated only when absolutely necessary and because . . . *It would only be one kiss. One. Just enough to find out if being with him would have been as good as I've imagined it.* "I've never heard of that custom."

He traced the line of her jaw with the back of one of his fingers. "It might only be mine." He leaned in until his lips were just above hers.

Josephine swayed and her eyes began to close. *One taste then I leave. Just one little indulgence.*

Gabe's phone rang in the breast pocket of his jacket. He let it ring through, looped his hands behind her waist, and pulled her against him. In a deep, sexy voice he said, "It's my first time implementing it." His phone rang again and he groaned. "I don't want to answer it, but it could be something to do with my family. Some of them are taking my father's passing hard."

"Of course," she whispered back and would have moved away, but he held her to his side. *What am I doing? This is not the plan. This is exactly how to screw up the plan.* She let him hold her while he reached for his phone, though, because every part of him felt so damn good. *How is that possible? We're both still dressed, but my skin is on fire. Oh, God, if it gets better than this I may not say no.*

Gabe frowned when he looked at the caller ID then held his phone to his head. "Now is not a good time."

Josephine wasn't trying to listen in, but she heard a man answer. "Understood, but we need more time. We haven't found anything yet."

"Nothing?"

"We have not yet been able to find a Josie Arlington who matches your description in the age range you gave us."

Gabe looked down at her as if checking if she could hear. She kept her face carefully blank even though she was pretty sure she was about to throw up from nerves. *He's having me investigated? Shit. Shit. Double shit.*

I don't have money for lawyers.

Without proof of my innocence, they'll put me in prison and take my research.

I can't stay here.

I can't leave without my lab equipment. I don't have the funds to purchase everything again, but I can't pack it up while he's here.

Shit.

Why can't I be the kind of person who could kill someone?

Or at least knock him out.

"We found one Josie Arlington in the area, but she was eighty-six years old, and she died last week," the man on the phone said.

Is that where I came up with the name? I must have seen the obituary. Oh, my God. I'm getting sloppy.

"I'll call you with more tomorrow," Gabe said abruptly and hung up. His expression was unreadable. He ran a hand up and down one of her arms in a caress, but stopped and looked down at her. "Is your tattoo fake?"

SHE WENT TO pull away from him but he grabbed her upper arm and held her still as he studied it. *Real tattoos don't flake off beneath the touch.* Her stance changed as if she were preparing for another physical battle.

"I like tattoos, but not enough to commit to one. Is that a crime?" She tried to yank her arm away from him.

He waited for her to stop struggling then released her arm. "Not as far as I know." His joke fell flat.

She stepped back from him. "Thanks for dinner."

He stayed where he was because she looked cornered. That wasn't the reaction he'd hoped she'd have to spending time with him. "Do you really want to leave?"

Her eyes flashed with a hunger that matched the one burning inside him, but then she looked away. "It's for the best."

"Spend tomorrow with me."

She shook her head. "I would, but I have so much I need to do."

Interesting. "Anything I could help you with?"

"No. No. Just need to clean up a few things." She crossed the room with ego-bruising speed.

"Dinner?"

She glanced over her shoulder as she started to open the door. "Maybe. Depends on how much I get done. Sorry."

From beside her he said, "Don't be. I'm here to evaluate the condition of the house and grounds. I'll do that while you get your work done. Take my phone number and call me when you finish."

Her hand tightened on the door knob and for just a split second he would have sworn she looked scared. *Of me?* His gut clenched. He was ruthless in business, but not with women—never with them. He touched her shoulder gently. "Hey. You can say no. It won't change our deal. You can still stay until the place sells."

She kept her face averted then turned, and the plea in her eyes knocked the breath clear out of him. "Two years. It's been two years since I've been on a date."

He swayed toward her, drawn in a way that defied all logic. "And you're scared."

She turned, with her hands holding the door behind her. Open to him. Vulnerable and so damn beautiful he could barely think. "Can we take things slowly? I'm not really good at this."

"This?"

"Whatever we're doing."

He raised his hand to her cheek. Reassuring her took top priority. "We can go as slowly as you need." *Although, hopefully, slowly wraps up by Sunday around noon.*

She let out a shaky breath. "I'd like to spend tomorrow with you, but not here. Can we go somewhere?"

"Where would you want to go?"

She took his hand in her warm one. "How about I surprise you?"

He wasn't a man who liked surprises, but if it meant spending the day with her, he was in. "Sounds perfect."

"We'll leave early."

"Don't you have things you need to do?"

She let go of his hand and raised her thumb, running it ever so lightly across his bottom lip. "I'll do them on Sunday after you leave."

Her touch felt so damn good.

His blood headed south in a rush, and he wanted nothing more than to devour that sweet mouth of hers, but he didn't. She'd asked for time and she was sure as hell worth waiting for. "Good."

"I do have one request, though."

"Anything," he answered in a strangled voice.

Her hand traced his chin then dropped to the knot of his tie. "Tomorrow, lose the tie."

She turned and darted out the door before he had a chance to say he would. In a gloriously painful state of excitement, he stood there, watching her go. He didn't move until she paused at the door of the guest house and waved before going in.

He waved back, closed the door, and walked into his father's study. Josie's absence affected his mood as much as her presence did. He wanted to walk across the driveway, bang on the door until she opened it, and simply be with her. Naked. Dressed. Talking. Silent. It didn't matter. He needed more of her.

This isn't like me. I've never minded being alone. I don't need anyone.

After pouring himself a Bushmills 21year single malt, he pulled his tie off and tossed it on his father's desk. His father had been with a fair share of women in the years after his mother had died. *I'll have to decide about the ranch next weekend, Dad. I'm sure you understand.*

Feeling too restless to consider sleeping, Gabe reached for his laptop and dug in to his work. The challenge of work always made him feel better. It was the place where things made sense to him. *Did Dad feel the same after Mom died?*

Before I came here I thought I'd become a man you'd be proud of. In every way I thought mattered, I was winning.

The expansion couldn't have come at a better time. His team was strong. His network was solid. *But is that all I am?*

Nothing would fall apart if he stepped away for a weekend. His evening with Josie hadn't ended the way he'd hoped, but somehow that was even better. Most things came too easily to him. Women. Success. It was too easy to take both for granted.

Josie was different. Nothing about her was easy or predictable.

He considered calling back the security company, but he didn't have anything new to tell them.

Except that I can now imagine myself spending several weekends down here. Gabe took a healthy swig and raised the glass in salute. *You were right, Luke. There are some things that are worth putting time aside for.*

Chapter Four

LATER THAT NIGHT, Josephine packed in preparation for bolting. It was easy since she had very few personal items. Once done, she showered, took out her contacts, and put on a nightgown her father had given her a few years back for her birthday. It had a high neckline and fell to her ankles. She remembered laughing and asking him if he realized she was no longer a child.

In his gentle authoritative voice, he'd said, "You're never too old to be modest."

She'd only kept it because he hadn't given her many gifts, and he'd obviously chosen the nightgown himself. When she wore it, she felt he was with her. *I never realized how much I relied on you, Dad. In all the times we relocated, were you ever afraid?*

I am.

I'm afraid I will fail you.

Afraid I might discover your death was my fault. Were you trying to prove something to me? Is that why you were on the bike that day? Did you keep something from me? I don't understand what happened. What did I miss?

If you were here you'd tell me not to blame myself, but how can I not?

I convinced you the private sector was less dangerous than staying in the Army.

She buried her face in her hands. Aloud, she whispered, "What if I don't have the answers, Dad? What if I'm not as brilliant as you always said I was?"

I ran, Dad. Now some say I'm a criminal.

The worst part?

I'm beginning to feel like one.

You lost your life for this project and what am I doing? I'm sitting here mourning the loss of a man I just met.

It's probably a good thing I'm leaving this ranch. Six months doesn't sound long, but it is when you're alone. Weeks pass without me talking to anyone. No wonder I wish . . . She raised her head and wiped a stray tear. *Nothing. It's better to wish for nothing.* She stood and walked back to the living room where her computer was.

After tomorrow I'm gone. She plopped on her couch with a notepad and her laptop and used an alias along with a prepaid credit card to secure a moving truck for late Sunday night. Untraceable. *There will be no trace I was ever here.*

I'll simply disappear.

She made a quick list of what she'd need. *Red hair this time? Green contacts? No tats. I can be an unemployed waitress running from an abusive relationship. Or a frustrated writer looking for a quiet place to finish a book.*

I need a monthly rental. Somewhere within driving distance in case I forget something here.

I won't forget anything.

Would black hair be less memorable? I can't stand out. I need to be forgettable. She leaned back and closed her eyes. *With Gabe, too. He can't look for me after I've gone.*

He can probably have any woman he wants, and I'm worried that he'll try to find me after I leave? It won't be a problem.

There was a firm knock on the door to the guest house that startled Josephine into almost dropping her laptop. She put it to the side and stood. She normally took her gun with her, but she'd left it in the toolbox. *Because I'm distracted, and that's dangerous.* "Who is it?"

"Gabe. I saw your light on. It's a beautiful night out here. I thought you might like to sit out on the swing with me."

Her heart raced, and even though she knew she should say no, she wavered. She walked to the door, but didn't open it. "I'm already dressed for bed."

"Throw a jacket on if you're not decent." His voice was light with humor. "Or don't."

Josephine looked down. She was more covered up than she had been in her day clothes. *If I'm looking for a way to show him I'm not a femme fatale, this should work.* She opened the door.

Although Gabe had taken off his suit jacket, he was still in the same trousers and light gray shirt. His sleeves were rolled up, though, and the top few buttons of his shirt were undone. She had a feeling he was the rare man who became better looking the more clothes he took off. *I wish I could find out.* She fought an urge to run her hands across his broad chest and bury them in his still perfectly groomed hair. He whistled and said, "That's quite a nightgown."

She raised her chin proudly. "My father gave it to me."

"Before or after he chased your dates off with a shotgun?" Gabe asked with a chuckle.

"My father didn't require a weapon. Just a look from him sent most of them scurrying away."

Gabe nodded in approval. "Sounds like my kind of man." He looked her over again. "And you wear it well."

"Thank you." He sounded sincere. She closed the door behind her and lingered in front of it.

"Come on." He held out a hand for her to take.

She hesitated.

His smile was gentle. "I heard you earlier. No pressure. You can trust me."

She couldn't. Not with the truth, but it was tempting to pretend for a moment that she was simply a woman agreeing to sit out beneath the stars with a man she liked. Would it be so wrong to let herself have this little piece of happiness? She placed her hand in his and lied. "I do."

"Good." He tucked her hand in the crook of his arm and walked down the steps with her, toward the main house. "If I remember correctly my father hung the swing so he and my mother could sit out and watch the stars."

"Sounds like he loved her very much."

"He did. She was the only person who could get him

to stop long enough to enjoy a place like this." Gabe held the porch swing still while Josephine sat, then he joined her. He placed his arm across the back of the chair and eased her against him. "Comfortable?"

She nodded, barely breathing. She was exquisitely aware of every place their bodies touched. From the heat of his thigh against hers to the solid strength of his chest along her side.

He pointed at a bright point in the night sky. "If I'm right, that's Venus."

It was Mars, but Josephine wasn't about to correct him. He could make up a new name for every constellation and all she would care about was how good it felt to be tucked into his side.

As he absently played with the lace on the sleeve of her nightgown, he said, "I forgot how amazing the sky is out here. My brothers and I used to go out on the lawn with telescopes while my parents sat here. I can see why they loved this spot. Even here, the stars look close enough to touch." He chuckled. "Who knows, maybe we'll see the space station."

Relaxing against him, Josephine said, "The ISS has an orbital inclination of fifty-one point sixty-five degrees. It completes one orbit in roughly ninety-three minutes, but that would only be observable at night and, depending on its position relative to that of the sun, infrequently. It has passed over this area, but factoring in the changes in the ground track as it shifts westward and the variation in length of days over a calendar year, I'd say seeing it tonight is possible but highly improbable." Gabe frowned down at her as if she'd suddenly become a puzzle to him, and she realized she'd relaxed too much. She rounded her eyes, smiled brightly, and said, "I like the science channel."

His eyes held hers and he frowned more. "Are your eyes blue?"

Oh, shit. I'm not wearing my contacts. "Yes."

"Were they blue when we met?"

She wasn't about to tell him they hadn't been. "That's an odd question."

"I remember thinking you had beautiful dark eyes."

She stiffened and shifted away from him. "You're confusing me with someone else. How flattering for me."

He caught her chin in his hand and held it, forcing her to look up at him again. "I have to be more tired than I thought. I don't know why I thought they were brown, but, believe me, I haven't thought of another woman since we met. In fact, I'm finding it difficult to come up with coherent conversation when all I can think about is how much I want to kiss you."

Oh, yes. Yes, please.

She pulled her face away and gave herself an internal shake. *What am I doing? I need to end this now while I still mean nothing to him.*

He took her hand in his and laid it on his thigh. "But I won't. It may kill me, but I'm waiting for *you* to kiss *me.*"

She studied his expression. He meant it. He would

wait for her to make the first move. She didn't trust many people, but for some reason, she felt she could trust him. He seemed like a man who stood by what he said. That was more than could be said for most of her so-called friends who had claimed to care about her but had instantly believed the worst of her when Raymean had accused her of taking their designs. "You'll wait a while."

He smiled. "I'd expect nothing less from a woman in that nightgown."

She didn't want to like him, but she found herself starting to, and it scared her. He was strong and confident, but that wasn't what drew her to him the most. There was integrity beneath his ambitious veneer. He also had a sense of humor when it came to himself that tore right through her defenses and made her want to forget about everything else and smile along with him. There was so much she didn't know about him, so much she wanted to. She half hoped she'd discover something awful about him, something that would make it easier to walk away from him. She half hoped she wouldn't, because even if nothing came of it, it was nice to think that someone like him was possible. Improbable, like viewing the ISS on a random evening beneath the stars. "You said you had a renovation team. Are you in construction?"

His hand tightened on hers. "Real estate. What did you do before you came here?"

I shouldn't have asked a personal question. It opened the

door for him to do the same. "Do?"

"For a job."

The best cover stories were loosely based on the truth. Those were easiest to remember. "I worked with my father."

"On?"

"Odd jobs here and there."

He ran a hand up and down her arm in a light caress. "What kind of work was it?"

Josephine tilted her head up at the sky. "Do you see the light just below the moon? That's Saturn. People think of it as the only planet with rings, but that's incorrect. All the giant gas planets have them, but they're thin and nearly impossible to see. Rock planets like Earth and Mars don't have rings."

His hand stilled on her arm. "Are you in some kind of trouble?"

She removed her hand from his leg and shifted away from him again. "Of course not."

"Then why so secretive?"

"I'm not. Listen we only met today. I'm sorry if I'm not ready to spill my whole life to you."

He looked at her for a long moment. "You're right. I'm pushing." He paused, then added, "I have a confession to make."

"You do?" She swallowed hard. *Is this where he admits he is having me investigated? Demands to know the truth about me?*

"I've never liked surprises. I'm good at what I do

because I make sure I have all the facts before I make a move. I came to see you tonight because I have a question for you."

Oh, God. "You do?" *Breathe. I can't let him see I'm scared. I can talk my way out of whatever he asks if I stay calm.*

"Where are we going tomorrow? I only brought suits with me. If you want to do anything outdoors, I should stop somewhere and get more appropriate clothing."

He's worried about not having the right attire for our day together? Relief flooded through Josephine. She started to laugh so hard tears poured down her cheeks.

Her reaction seemed to confuse him. "It's a legitimate question. My brother Hunter says I'm not as adventurous as he is. I am, but let's be honest, hiking isn't going to happen in Stephano Bemers."

The more she laughed, the more offended he started to look. She didn't have the words or the courage to explain her reaction, but she gave in to an impulse and kissed his adorably pursed mouth.

THERE WEREN'T TOO many times in his life when Gabe could say he'd truly been taken by surprise. This was one of them. He had still been trying to determine if she was laughing or crying and what he'd said that would inspire either from her then—wham. Her lips were on his and all thinking stopped.

He pulled her across his lap and deepened their kiss with a hunger unlike any he'd experienced. Nothing mattered beyond the feel of her in his arms, her mouth opening to his, her arms sliding up around his neck. She was as sweet as he'd imagined and as bold. Her tongue danced with his as she buried a hand in the back of his hair.

He kissed his way to her ear then down to the high neckline of her gown. Her ragged breathing urged him on. Through the thick material of her gown he caressed her breast. Wanting more of her, he ran his hand down her leg, seeking the hem. When the cloth went on and on he thought of the man who had bought it for her and came abruptly back to reality with a chuckle. "Your father chose your sleepwear well. I feel like a teenager sneaking a kiss and feeling guilty about it."

Desire burned in her eyes, but she buried her face in his neck. "I'm an idiot. I shouldn't have kissed you; I'm not ready for this. I just can't think straight around you."

"I am similarly affected." He hugged her to his chest and let out a long, calming breath. With her position across his lap there was no need to say what he wanted. Proof of his need for her was prominent, and he enjoyed every time she shifted against it. Still, he was a man, not a boy. With age came control and the ability to distinguish recreational sex from complicated sex. Josie wasn't the type of woman a man had once and walked away from. She would require sex to come packaged in some level of relationship. At least, that was his impression of her.

But I don't know because I met her today.

Today.

I should be taking her out to dinner, asking her what her favorite wine is. I shouldn't be holding her like I've known her forever. She shifted her ass, and he groaned with pleasure. Letting his body, rather than common sense, decide how to proceed with her was dangerous. It didn't care that he knew next to nothing about her. It wanted to hold her, own her, give itself over to her.

Too much. Too fast.

But so damn good I don't want the weekend to end.

"I should go," she said softly.

"You should," he said, but didn't move to release her. He tucked her head beneath his chin and simply held her, gently running a hand through her long hair.

"This doesn't mean—"

"I know." He kissed the top of her head.

She sighed and relaxed against his chest. "I wish you weren't so nice. I don't want to like you."

He laughed at that. "Would it help if I said I don't want to like you either, but my dick finds you irresistible?"

ANOTHER WOMAN MIGHT have been offended, but she arched one of her eyebrows with a straight face and said, "It has good taste."

He swatted her bottom lightly and she laughed. In that moment he could imagine her in his house, his bed, sharing coffee with him before work. It was an uncomfortably vivid image that shook him.

Josie touched the side of his face gently. "What's wrong?"

"Nothing," he said, amazed at how she was more attuned to his mood than women he'd dated for months. Their connection was new, but real. He needed to lighten the mood. "So, what did you decide you want to do tomorrow?"

"There is a place in town that rents ATVs. Would you be interested in seeing some of the area?"

"I grew up here," he answered automatically and regretted not considering how she'd take it.

"Oh, of course. There isn't much as far as entertainment around here, but we could go for a hike. Or sit on the beach at the lake for a bit. It's beautiful there. If there's time, there is a new museum that was built last year."

"Full day." It sounded as though she was trying to keep both of them busy, which might not be such a bad idea. As she spoke, though, he realized that almost everything she wanted to do was possible on the ranch. Memories of swimming with his brothers in the run-off creek down in the valley brought a nostalgic smile to his lips. There was one spot in it that was almost deep enough for diving. He wondered if the rope still hung from the tree beside it. It suddenly felt important to revisit the places that had brought him happiness as a child, and he wanted Josie at his side when he did. "My father always kept ATVs in the garage. They're probably still there. Why don't we take them down into the valley?

I'm here to see the property one last time. I might as well see all of it."

Her smile looked strained. "That makes sense."

He cursed himself for bringing up the sale of the ranch. She was probably worried about where she'd go next. "Josie, no matter what happens with this place, I'll make sure—" He stopped because he didn't know what the hell he could promise her. "It'll be at least a month before anything happens."

She nodded. "I'll be fine."

Not sure how to make her feel better and not ready to offer more than letting her stay until the sale, he said, "I'm heading to town early and picking up a few things. Do you want to join me?"

She blinked a few times as she considered his offer. "No. I'll sleep in. What time do you think you'll be back?"

"Ten?"

"I'll be ready." She slid off his lap, and he let her go.

He stood as she darted down the steps. He opened his mouth, then closed it because he didn't want her to leave, but he sure as hell didn't want to say it. The outline of her rushing across the driveway in her long nightgown reminded him of a cover on some historical novel. Everything about meeting her was surreal enough that he could be convinced he'd crashed his car on the drive down and was actually in a coma, dreaming.

She stopped just before entering the guest house and waved. There was no light behind her, nothing revealed by her very chaste nightgown, but that didn't stop him from imagining every inch of her—vividly. Still sporting a boner, he waved back. Ending the night early had been the right thing to do, but that didn't make it any easier to watch her go.

Complicated.

Chapter Five

A T EIGHT THIRTY the next morning, Gabe drove
down the driveway and Josephine sprinted to her
hidden lab in the main garage. She didn't let herself
think about the night before or how tenderly he'd held
her after their kiss. If she were going to survive this, she
needed to remain focused.

She knew she wouldn't be able to pack everything in
the hour and a half he'd be gone, so she decided to
remove just the bike and computers. She drove the bike
to the guest house and stashed it in one of the bedrooms.
She boxed her server and desktop computers and
shuttled each container to closets in the guest house.
Time flew by too quickly. It was a quarter to ten by the
time she stashed her fifth load into the hallway closet.

She swore when she heard the sound of car tires on
the gravel. A quick look in the mirror confirmed her
fears. She was sweaty and flushed. No way would he
believe she just woke up. She bolted for the shower and
calmed her nerves beneath a cool spray.

Images of Gabe kept popping into her head, and she
kept pushing them away. She tingled all over whenever

she thought of how good it had felt to sit with him, to feel his strong thigh beneath her hand. *I was tired last night and feeling sorry for myself. Add a dash of lonely and that explains why I kissed him. It doesn't mean anything, and I'm lucky he didn't take it as an invitation for more. Now I just need to keep him out of the garage. He lived here. He's going to notice the wall I put up.*

The ATVs.

Shit.

I forgot to move them to the driveway. Crap.

She threw on jeans, a T-shirt, and tennis shoes. A peek out the window confirmed he was already back in the main house with his purchases. *Maybe I can beat him there.* She threw her damp hair into a ponytail and rushed out of the guest house.

She came to a skidding stop when she saw him walking across the driveway toward her. The smile that spread across his face at the sight of her sent her heart into a crazy beat. She found herself smiling back despite the panic welling within her.

"Morning," he said lazily. "I am now officially ready for anything." He referenced his casual attire.

Me, too.

Gabe in a suit was gorgeous. Gabe in jeans was decadent. The tan cotton of his shirt highlighted his muscular shoulders and flat stomach. The jeans were just tight enough to show off his amazing thighs. Her eyes skimmed over the part of him that had befuddled her brain the night before and could almost feel it's delicious hardness pulsing against her derriere. It seemed to be growing again beneath her gaze. She tore her eyes upward to meet his. "Good morning." Her voice sounded breathless and excited.

He closed the distance between them and cupped her face between both of his hands. "It is good." His kiss was brief, but toe-curling. When he lifted his head she wanted nothing more than to pull his mouth back to hers, but she didn't. There was still a small sliver of sanity in her, and she clung to it rather than him.

Think. You can do this. "We should probably take bottled water with us. Do you have any in the house?"

"I do." He looked mildly disappointed by her reaction to the kiss.

Too bad. We can't all have what we want, can we? "If you get the water, I'll take the ATVs out."

He frowned then nodded. "I'll be right back."

Josephine drove one ATV out of the garage in record time. She would have had the second one out, but it didn't start. *Shit.* She scrambled to check if it had gas. It did. She tried to start it again. Nothing.

Gabe walked into the garage just as she was looking around for a third option. He stood in the middle of the garage and said, "Isn't it amazing how different everything looks when you're young? I used to think this garage was enormous, but it's not."

Before he looked too closely at why, Josephine knew she had to get him out of there. She rushed to his side and led him toward the ATV in the driveway. "Yes, amazing. I knew one of the ATVs worked because I've seen Frank out on it, but the other one was dead. We'll have to share."

His easy smile returned. "I'll suffer through somehow." He placed the waters in a saddlebag on the back of the vehicle and climbed onto it. "The gas tank is full. Let's test it out."

Josephine climbed on behind him. She held on to his sides, but left a distance on the seat between them.

"I almost forgot something," he said and hopped off the vehicle with an agility that revealed how comfortable he'd once been on one.

Josephine held her breath as she watched him stride back into the garage. *It's nothing. He doesn't suspect anything.*

"I don't want you to get killed on our second date." He tossed a helmet to her and put one on himself. "If I remember right, some of the trails are rocky. Safety is never a bad idea."

He slid back in front of her and she gripped his sides again. *I'm trying. I'm trying to play it safe, but it's not easy.*

Sexy and he cares about my safety? He's what I've been missing.

He didn't drive like a man who waited for all the information before making a move. He flew down the driveway and across the field at a speed that took her by surprise. Speed didn't scare her, but the combination of wild abandon and rocky terrain was enough to almost send her tumbling off the back. She wrapped her arms around him, plastered herself to his back, and held on for dear life.

He stopped at the beginning of one of the trails. "My brothers and I rode every inch of this ranch a hundred times over. I forgot how fun it can be."

"Says the man with an Aston Martin."

He smiled back at her. "That was a gift I have every intention of using as an investment piece, after I fix the ding."

"Where's the fun in that?"

His eyes held hers for a long moment. "Fun hasn't been a priority of mine since," he scanned his memories, "since I left here."

"When your mother died."

His muscles rippled beneath her touch. "Yes. She loved the ranch and made it a magical place for all of us. Strange, I haven't thought much about her or the ranch until I came back here. I guess I closed the door on that part of my life."

Josephine's hold around his waist became a full body hug. She understood all too well how sometimes going on required shutting a piece of yourself down. Otherwise, loss simply hurt too much. "You don't sound like you want to sell it."

He laid a hand over one of hers. "I have time to make that decision. My parents loved this place so much, they had their ashes buried in the canyon. Do you mind if we swing by there? I don't want to bring down the mood of the day, but I'd like to see the site."

She hugged him tighter. *There are deeper levels to this man than I thought.* "I would, too."

With that, he twisted the right-hand throttle and they were flying down the path at the same crazy speed they'd taken over the lawn. This time, though, Josephine saw the ride through his eyes. He was reliving a happier time in his life and taking her along. It was beautifully touching in a bumpy, hold-on-or-you'll-go-flying-off way.

Holding on was what she feared she might do.

She'd always been able to walk away. Move away. Start again. Assume a new role. *But it had always been with my dad. Never alone.* What would it be like to actually stay? What would it be like to come home to someone? *That's a silly thought, Josephine. That's not in my future. Tomorrow I have to let go of him . . . aware of the crazy fantasy that someone like me could have someone like him in my life. If I really were Josie Arlington would a weekend together become two? Because spending time with him is exhilarating. Would this attraction grow into love? Marriage? Two children, a dog, and holidays with his family?*

None of that is possible no matter how tight I hold on. It's not real.

It's not me.

IF HIS BROTHERS had told him he would be flying down dirt trails acting like he was twenty years younger, he would have asked them what they'd been drinking. This wasn't the way he behaved. Ever.

Yet, somehow, it felt right.

Gabe thought back to the day his aunt had called him to say his father had died. He'd gone back to work after hearing the news and later gone to see his brothers. The sadness he'd expected at the loss hadn't come. That wasn't something he could say aloud without sounding like he didn't love his father. *I did love him; we simply weren't a big part of each other's lives.*

Perhaps it was because he and Josie were headed toward where his parents' ashes were, but Gabe suddenly felt the loss deeply. He was momentarily transported back to a summer when his mother was alive. The four oldest boys—James, Gabe, Hunter, and Max—were farther down the trail on one ATV, racing to keep up with their mother, while the three youngest had stayed back at the house with Aunt Claire. The destination had been the canyon because it was their mother's favorite place. When they stopped on the grassy area near the river that cut through the canyon, their mother had smiled and said it was so beautiful it must be a little piece of heaven that had fallen to earth.

You shouldn't have left your heaven to me, Dad. I don't own anything I wouldn't sell for the right price. You chose poorly if you thought I'd be the one to keep this place in our family.

The ATV went over a rock and tilted to one side. Josie's arms tightened around his waist and the past drifted away. "Having fun?" he asked over the roar of the engine.

"I haven't hit the dirt yet, so—yes," she answered with a laugh.

He slowed the vehicle and the euphoria that had come from speeding down the trail was replaced by an equally enjoyable awareness of her body clinging to his. Her thighs warmed the outside of his. Her breasts bounced against his back. There were definitely worse ways to spend a Saturday. "See the tree over there? The one with the three low branches?"

"Are you going to drive up it?" she joked.

He stopped the ATV and looked back at her, pretending to be offended. "What are you implying?"

She laughed. "Only that some people avoid obstacles for the comfort of their passengers."

"Think you can do better? Want to drive back from the canyon?" The idea of reversing their positions was a tantalizing one.

"You're on," she said in a husky tone that made him wonder if she was looking forward to the ride back for the same reason he was. She pointed at the tree he'd mentioned. "What were you saying about the tree?"

He was having trouble remembering. Once he imagined her gorgeous little ass moving up and down against him, it was difficult to think at all. He shook his head. "I broke my arm on that tree. Hunter was near the top, convinced it was the best view on the ranch. I told him to take a picture of it because there was no way in hell I was climbing up that spindly tree. He dared me, and to make a long story short, I wore a cast the rest of the summer."

She laughed again. "At least you proved you weren't afraid of climbing."

"What I proved was that my instincts about the reliability of those branches to hold the weight of two people was sound. I've never been one to leap before fully evaluating where I'd land. Hunter is the exact opposite. He charges ahead sometimes with no idea of what he's running into. He's been lucky so far, but some falls can be game changers."

She tensed behind him. "It's not always possible to know what lies around the corner. I wish it were. I don't like the unknown either, but sometimes it's all we have."

Was she referring to how little they knew about each other or her uncertainty about where she'd go after the ranch sold? "You keep saying you'll be fine when you leave here. Where will you go?"

Her silence was unsettling. Either she didn't know or she didn't want to tell him. He didn't like either possibility. He twisted the throttle and took off down the trail again. He and Josie weren't lovers. They weren't even friends yet. Where she went and who she went with was none of his business.

Do I want it to be?

I've spent a lifetime keeping my life simple, focused—even in my personal life. I enjoy people while they are with me, but I don't hold on to relationships any more than I hold on to properties.

He was practical to the core.

He'd never owned a house he'd considered *his*. His address changed depending on projects he worked on. His relationships were the same. His last name along with his financial status was enough to guarantee a steady flow of interested women. He was a man in his prime with a healthy appetite for sex, and short-term, casual relationships provided that. He didn't ask a woman who she'd been with last and didn't care who she went with after him. *He'd never cared.*

THERE WAS VERY little chance that a woman of Josie's age, somewhere in her mid-twenties, was a virgin. *So, who had she been with? Had they been good to her? Was one of them the reason she kept so much to herself?* He didn't like that she felt she needed a gun.

Were any of them someone she intended to turn to when she left the ranch? His stomach tightened at that thought. He'd never been a jealous man, but he didn't like the idea of her with anyone else. He had no idea how being with Josie for less than twenty-four hours had caused such a protective streak, especially given they'd only stolen a few kisses. *Even the six months with whatshername in wheresitsplace never inspired this indefinable urge.*

Those thoughts were broken when Gabe and Josie reached the bottom of the canyon. A white stone bench stood as the marker where his parents' ashes were buried. Gabe parked the ATV a few feet away from it then waited as Josie got off first. He joined her beside the bench.

"It's so beautiful here," she said in a tone full of wonder.

He looked down at the bench engraved with his parents' names. Regardless of where his father had gone after his mother's death, he had returned to her in the end. *Is this what you wanted me to see, Dad? That Mom always owned your heart? That family is what matters? If so, I hope you sent the same message to the other six. If you want me to believe you were this sentimental, it's going to be a hard sell. How many phone calls were you too busy to return? I never judged you for it, but now . . . If it's your aim for me to become the family man you weren't, it's not going to happen.*

He pictured his mother shaking her head, reminding him to be respectful of his father. He could see her turning to his father, as she often had, and reminding him to be equally as respectful toward his son. *"It's easy to get caught up in what matters the least and forget what matters the most."* His mother had held her husband and her boys in check with love rather than force. When he scanned the creek and the grassy area that flanked it, he forgot to ask himself what that view would be worth to a potential buyer. Instead he let the memories from the many happy times he'd spent there wash over him. "It *is* beautiful."

He looked across at Josie who seemed to be lost in her thoughts as well. She didn't wear makeup or dress seductively. When she spoke, it wasn't to flirt with sexual innuendos. She was genuine and as striking as the backdrop behind her, real in a world that was all about appearances.

As he watched, she stepped out of her tennis shoes and rolled up the legs up her jeans. She walked into the creek then raised her eyes to his. With a mischievous smile on her face, she kicked an arc of water in his direction. It fell short of reaching him.

"You're lucky you missed," he said, advancing toward the water.

"Because Mr. Fancy Pants is afraid to get wet?" she parried playfully.

Gabe stepped out of his shoes. The creek became much deeper a few feet beyond where she stood. Because of the rock formation downstream the current was never overly powerful. He and his brothers had gone swimming in that very spot every summer. He lifted his shirt over his head and dropped it beside his shoes. Her mouth rounded and her eyebrows rose. The way her gaze lingered on his bare chest was an added bonus. He undid the button of his jeans and her jaw fell open when he stepped out of them as well. His smile was wide and wicked when he straightened in a pair of bathing trucks. "I'm ready. Kick some water in my direction again."

"Don't you dare. I didn't wear a bathing suit." She backed away, toward where the creek dropped and raised a hand in defense.

He took a step in her direction. "So sad. What are you going to do? Get all your clothing wet or take them off?"

She retreated again. "How about we agree that I stay completely dry?"

He advanced. "That option disappeared when you attempted to douse me."

"I missed."

He bent and cupped his hand, preparing to splash her. "I won't."

Her eyes narrowed in challenge. "You will. I'm fast." She bolted backward and sank into the depth of the creek. He was beside her in a flash, wrapping an arm around her and pulling her with him to an area where he could stand.

She pushed her wet hair back from her face. He loved the laughter in her eyes as she swatted his arm. "You jerk. You could have warned me."

"I should have." The water wasn't cold enough to hide his reaction to her body settling against his. "With you, I forget to be careful."

Her hands clung to his shoulders. She bit her bottom lip and looked up at him with a mixture of yearning and sadness. "I can't forget. No matter how much I wish I could." She pushed away from him and found her own footing on the creek bed. "I'm sorry."

He'd never wanted a woman more than he wanted her right then, but he let her take another step away. "Are you married?"

"No," she said.

"Did someone hurt you?" *Would she tell me?*

"Yes, but not the way you probably think. Please just drop it." She made it back to the shallow area and stood with clothes plastered to her. It would have been a sight he would have enjoyed had she not looked so sad. "I wish . . ."

"What do you wish?" He went to stand beside her.

"It doesn't matter," she said and turned away.

He followed her to shore and gently turned her around then held her before him. "It does to me."

"I wish I hadn't met you," she said and turned away from him.

Chapter Six

IT WASN'T A kind thing to say, but Josephine's anger with herself was spilling over onto Gabe. She started up the trail that led back to the house. She wanted to laugh with him, splash in the water like carefree children. More than anything, she wanted to throw her arms around his neck, pull him down for a kiss, and spend the rest of the morning rolling around in the grass with him. Naked. Dressed. Wet. Dry. She'd take any scenario that included his lips on hers and those strong arms around her.

But I can't.

He doesn't even know my real name.

Why did he have to pursue me? Why do I want to trust him almost as much as I want to finish the power cell?

I used to believe in what I was doing. Now I don't know. I thought I could save my father, but I lost him anyway. I thought I could clear his name, but all I've done is hide and perpetuate the idea that we both might have been criminals.

When I had nothing else, I had my father's dream to fulfill.

I had a goal, and it didn't matter if I was alone. I was

used to being alone.

But now?

I want to tell Gabe everything. Confess like the fool I am.

And then what?

Beg him to believe me?

Why would he when my own friends didn't?

He has his own life, Josephine.

Gabe caught up to her and stopped her with a hand on her shoulder. "Whatever this is between us, it scares the hell out of me, too."

She turned and met his eyes. "I keep reminding myself I met you yesterday."

"I keep reminding myself you pulled a gun on me," he said dryly.

She shivered. "What are those instincts that told you the top of the tree was dangerous telling you now?"

He pulled her into his arms, warming her against his chest. "They're telling me I'll spend the rest of my life regretting walking away without doing this." His lips claimed hers in a kiss so tender Josephine forgot to be careful again.

It was so easy to give in to her hunger and kiss him back with equal passion. She told herself that everything wrong with her life would be waiting for her, but it didn't need to deprive her of this moment. *No one gets hurt as long as I don't let it go too far.* His hands dug into her hair, cradling her as he deepened the kiss. She slid her hands up his bare chest, knowing she should push him away, but unable to force herself to. His skin was warm and smooth. His muscles flexed beneath her touch. She fisted her hands against his chest. Desire and duty. Guilt and loneliness. Kissing him felt incredible and gut-wrenchingly painful at the same time.

She tore her mouth from his and brought her forehead down onto her clenched hands. He held her in his arms and rested his chin lightly on top of her head. She wanted to be honest with him about how she felt, but she was already lying to him about so much already. *I'm tearing myself up over this, but he'll probably forget me by Sunday night.*

"Look at me," he commanded softly.

She raised her eyes to his.

It would have been easy to walk away from him if he'd been annoyed that she'd stopped. Had he pushed, she could have told herself he was like every other man and only wanted one thing. Instead he gave her a lopsided smile that tugged at her heart. "I lose my head around you, but that doesn't mean I didn't hear what you said. We'll take this as slowly as you need to."

She pushed at him then, because the nicer he was the guiltier she felt. "I can't do this."

He tucked a lock of wet hair behind her ear. "I'd expect more courage from the firecracker who confronted me in the driveway yesterday."

"Don't talk to me about courage." She shoved him back then, and his arms fell to his sides. For a moment caution was tossed to the side and six months of struggle poured out. "I could have taken the easy route, but I didn't, and it cost me everything. So don't you dare tell me I lack courage. It's all I have left."

She knew instantly that she'd said too much. He towered over her. "What happened? What brought you here?"

Although she wanted to hide her face in her hands, she didn't allow herself that luxury. He wanted to help her. That wouldn't last, though, once he knew the truth about why she was there. He wouldn't believe her story any more than her friends had. She squared her shoulders and chose her words carefully. One lie layered easily over the others she had told him and hopefully would buy her time. "I'm not ready to talk about it yet, but maybe we could see each other after this weekend. I don't know, maybe you could come down again, or I could go see you. I'll tell you everything but not this weekend." *Like I always say, the best lies are based on the truth.* She had no intention of being at the ranch more than a few hours after he left. When he returned, if he returned, there would be no trace of her or where she'd gone. *He doesn't need to know that.*

"That sounds fair enough. Your clothes are soaked. Do you want to head back and change?" Genuine concern still darkened his eyes, and Josephine had to stop herself from stepping right back into the security of his embrace.

"Would you mind if I said yes?"

"I wouldn't have asked if I did."

"Then, yes. I'd like to get into some dry clothes." Unfortunately, it was still early enough in the day that she needed to find another way to occupy his time. "I'm hungry, are you?"

He seemed to rethink his first answer before saying, "Absolutely. Let's get the ATV and make lunch."

"Great. Then, if you want, I could show you some of *my* favorite spots on the ranch."

He offered her his hand as if to assist her. "I'd like that."

She placed her hand in his and they started down the way they came.

He laced his fingers with hers. "Whatever you're afraid of—you don't have to face it alone."

Josephine pressed her lips together and refused to give in to the emotions swirling within her. *That's where you're wrong, Gabe. Alone is all I'll ever be.* She couldn't afford to take time to mourn the loss of her dad, or feel sorry for herself, and the more she got to know Gabe the more she wanted to protect him from the mess she was in. *That's not how I'm wired and it's illogical to need to factor in another in my world . . . yet, I want that.*

Gabe Brannigan—why couldn't you be an asshole?

This would be so much easier if you weren't so damned likeable.

After donning his jeans and T-shirt again, Gabe thoroughly enjoyed riding behind Josie on the ATV. He tried to distract himself by creating a mental list of the work piling up for him back at his office. It didn't matter. He felt like a teenager sporting a boner during an exam. His ability to concentrate was shot but explaining why wouldn't help the situation.

When she pulled up to the front of the guest house, he hopped off, needing to put some distance between himself and her delectable derriere. If she was aware of how much he'd enjoyed the ride, she didn't call attention to it. She said, "I'll be quick."

"I'll meet you back here." It wouldn't take him long to change out of his swimming trunks.

"No," she said with a nervous wave of her hand. "I'll meet you at the main house."

He frowned. Was there a reason she didn't want him in the guest house? His thought must have been easy enough to read because she grimaced and said, "I was nervous about what to wear and tried on more clothes than I want to admit to. They're still all over the place. I hate people to see my place when it's a mess, don't you?"

Technically it was his place, but he kept that thought to himself, too. "That's fine. I'll have the chef from last night whip up a lunch." He hadn't taken her for the kind of woman who would be easily embarrassed, but the idea of having him in the guest house had definitely made her jumpy.

"He'll do that?"

"If I pay him enough."

She laughed as if he were joking, then stopped and smiled sheepishly. "Okay, sounds great. I really only want something simple like a salad with some chicken."

"You've got it," he said. "I'll have him prepare something for dinner while he's here."

"Dinner," she echoed hoarsely.

"Unless that's too much. My plan is to leave tomorrow morning. I'm enjoying our time together, but there's plenty for me to do if you need some time on your own."

The way she chewed her bottom lip indecisively was far from flattering. He was used to women competing for his attention. He couldn't remember a time when a woman had put so much thought into deciding if she wanted him.

He had to admit it was a turn-on.

No surprise there. With her, almost everything was.

"Dinner sounds wonderful," she said then turned and rushed into the guest house.

He stood in the driveway for several minutes after she left. Eventually, he turned and walked to the main house because the alternative was to still be standing there sporting a hard-on and grin simply because she'd said yes.

As he changed into the khaki pants and collared shirt he'd purchased earlier that day, he compared Josie to the women he normally chose. On paper, she wasn't his type. He tried and failed to imagine taking her to a fundraising gala or opening night of an opera.

If he brought her as is, his friends would think he'd lost his mind.

I can find new friends. Did I really just think that?

The chef arrived in record time, but that didn't surprise Gabe. Money was a powerful motivator for most people. As Gabe waited for Josie, he returned to his father's office and sat at his desk. *You could have raised us anywhere, Dad. Why did we spend so much time here? All those times I thought you were busy, were you really coping the best you could?*

His father had always been larger than life. He won because he wasn't afraid of the fight. Gabe had always thought of him as a man without weakness, the exact kind of man he'd wanted to grow up to be. And, to some degree, he had. But now he wondered. Was his opinion of his dad still determined by his twenty-year-old college-student self, idealizing his materialistic, emotionally void idol? *Not void at all. Hurting. Hiding. Is that why you wanted us to stay where Mom was even though you couldn't?*

Did you think we'd forget her? Forget who you were when you were with her? Gabe tried to open the middle drawer of his father's desk, but it was locked. He opened one of the side drawers, looking for a key. Instead, he found a framed photo of his father shaking hands with a man Gabe didn't recognize. He placed it on the desk and continued his hunt for a key.

A lower drawer revealed a ledger with Frank Muller's name on it. Inside was a supply list and sketches. The list included a CPU, circuit boards, tubes, a soldering kit, tin, wires and a three-dimensional printer. He flipped through the pages and found a loose, folded piece of paper. On it there was a sketch of something that looked like a beer keg but with a control panel on the front of it.

Holy shit, what was Frank involved in . . . instead of keeping up the grounds?

At the sound of a knock on the outer door, Gabe threw the ledger back in the drawer and stood. *Did you know what was going on here, Dad? Was that the reason for the occupancy clause? Did you want me to help him? Or was it to stop him?*

Once again, Dad, a note would have made all of this easier.

Before leaving the office, Gabe sent off a text to his security team. He wanted every bit of information they could dig up on Frank Muller.

As soon as he opened the front door and saw Josie's tentative smile, he put the ledger mystery on the backburner. Although she was once again dressed in jeans and a simple shirt, her cheeks were pink as if still warm from the shower. He wondered if there was anything she could wear that he wouldn't find sexy as hell. Her hair was down, and he fought an urge to bury his hands in it again. He didn't, but he couldn't resist leaning in for a quick kiss that took him by surprise with how natural it felt.

"Sorry I took so long," she said quickly.

"Right on time," he murmured and offered her his arm. "I had a table set on the patio."

She took his arm and smiled ruefully. "You're so formal. It makes me feel underdressed."

"Did you say *over*dressed?" he asked in a hopeful

tone, interjecting humor because she looked nervous. "Please feel free to take off whatever."

She rolled her eyes and nudged him with her elbow. "You'd like that, wouldn't you?"

He bent and growled into her ear. "No, I would *love* it."

She tripped, and he steadied her. "Gabe—"

"Trust me, Josie. Relax, enjoy today, and trust me."

She let out a shaky breath. "Okay."

Once they were settled outside, he poured her a glass of wine and said, "Tell me something about your childhood. Did you have an imaginary friend?"

She hesitated, then said, "No, but I did have dolls I took everywhere. I used to pretend they could speak so that's almost the same thing, I guess. Why, did you?"

If it required sharing more about himself to get her to open up, he would answer anything she asked. "I grew up with six brothers, I didn't need more friends, imaginary or otherwise. I treasured any moment I had to myself. Tell me, what kind of dolls were they?" He loved that he had no idea what she'd answer. Barbie and Ken? Something edgier?

She looked away for a moment as if reaching back into her memories, then she smiled. "They were a present from my father. One was Albert Einstein with a huge shock of white hair. The other was Niels Bohr with big bushy eyebrows. I loved to reenact their disputes on quantum physics. They had a great respect for each other, even though their ideas were sometimes in opposition. The beauty of their debates was how their discourse changed our very understanding of quantum mechanics and led to significant research into the hidden variables theory. Their disagreements were a gift to the world. I loved to imagine that I was there, hearing it all for the first time."

Silence. *Whoa.* "How old were you then?"

She shrugged. "Seven? Eight?"

"Holy shit. Are you serious?"

Her eyes rounded and for a second he thought he saw fear there. Then she smiled brightly and said, "No. *Of course not.* What seven-year-old knows anything about quantum physics? I was joking, but you believed me for a split second there, didn't you?"

"I did. You're good." He had, as ridiculous as it seemed once she'd admitted it was a joke. She was smart, but was she genius-level brilliant? Very few people were. "You sounded like you knew what you were talking about."

She raised and lowered a shoulder as if modestly shrugging off a compliment. "Like I said, I love the science channel."

"I'm going to have to watch myself with you. When you flash those baby blues at me I'm ready to believe anything you say."

She quickly blinked a few times at that, then her bright smile returned. "Then I should talk less, which works because I'm fascinated by what it must have been like to have six brothers. I'm an only child. Let me live vicariously through you. What was the best part? What were the holidays like? Did you fight? Did you ever accidentally date the same girls? I want all the dirt."

Of all the things women wanted to know about Gabe, those questions had never been asked. Josie was a constant, pleasant breath of fresh air. Gabe started with James, thinking he would briefly describe him and move on, but Josie asked question after question until she knew more about him than most of Gabe's friends did. Then she asked about Hunter and the cycle repeated. He didn't expect to make it to Finn. As the youngest, he'd sometimes been an afterthought, but Josie's interest in his family remained strong right through lunch. *It's as if she wants to know me, the family version of me, not the businessman. The man I thought had disappeared over the many years of business claiming first position in my priorities.* Like it had his dad.

→ "It must have been hard on your father to lose your mother when you were all still so young," she said.

"We had nannies."

"Still, that's a big responsibility."

"What about you?" Gabe asked. "What happened to *your* mother?"

She took a moment before answering. "I don't know. She told my father she wasn't ready to be a mother. She didn't want to marry or follow him. He told me that he'd heard she finally did marry and have a family, but she'd requested that I not contact her. Apparently, her husband doesn't know that she left me behind, and she wants it to stay that way."

Gabe didn't believe in hitting women, but if there were ever a woman in need of a slap it was that one. "She doesn't know what she's missing. Her daughter turned out amazing."

Josie shrugged again. "Thank you. It doesn't bother me anymore. My father loved me enough for both of them. And I don't know that I blame her. If the truth would destroy the perfect life she made for herself, maybe it's not worth it."

In her voice he heard, "Maybe *I'm* not worth it."

"I'm ready to hit the trails again. How about you?" Gabe threw down his napkin and stood. Her sadness and confusion tore through him. Was this why she couldn't be honest about what had brought her to the ranch? Her mother had abandoned her. Had some man abused her? Did she feel she somehow deserved it? Or that he would walk away from her too if she told him? He wanted to shake her and tell her he wasn't going anywhere.

But I'm not ready to make that promise.

I just met her, for God's sake.

And I'm leaving tomorrow.

I don't have a month to give this place.

Or her.

She joined him with that uncertain look in her eye again that made him want to hug her to his chest. "If you don't mind, I'll just freshen up quickly before we go."

He let out a long sigh once he was alone. Desire muddled his thoughts. He'd never allowed a woman to impact his business, but because Josie had him all tied up in knots, he didn't know if he wanted to stay or leave that night.

If he thought having sex with her would lessen her hold over him, he would have given her a nudge in that direction. Despite her claim that it wasn't what she wanted, the heat in her kiss said it wouldn't take much to change her mind.

And then what?

Do I take her home with me?

Stay here with her and keep the ranch?

Both of those possibilities sound insane to me.

So why do I wish they didn't?

Chapter Seven

J OSIE GAVE HERSELF a stern look in the mirror. *He's not as perfect as he sounds. No one is. Everyone seems amazing before I get to know them.*

I'm not on a date.

None of this really matters.

I need to keep my mouth shut and stick to the plan. He leaves tomorrow. I leave tomorrow. We'll never see each other again, and we're both better for it.

I don't want to leave. There, I said it. I don't want to never see Gabe again. She turned and hugged her stomach while leaning back against the sink. *My father would say I should follow my heart, but it shattered when he died. How do I know if what I'm feeling is real or if I'm just looking for someone to be with? Of course I don't want to be alone. It would be wonderful to tell Gabe I'm afraid and hear him say everything will be okay.*

I can't burden him with my problems. It'll put him at risk. I used to think I had all the answers. I don't. I never did.

Dad, my heart is scattered in a million pieces. Which one do I follow?

Josephine turned and faced her reflection again.

Make it through today and tomorrow will be easier. Feeling calmer, Josephine went to meet Gabe. He shot her a smile that sent flutters through her stomach.

Please pick your nose.

Or make some disgusting noise in your throat.

I'm asking for a little flaw. Something.

"Ready? I'm looking forward to seeing your favorite places. I can't decide, though, if I should drive the ATV or if you should. Is it wrong to admit that both are different forms of sweet torture?"

Oh yes.

And—oh no.

From flutter to flame. His words lit through her. She knew exactly how decadent each option was. Did she want to spend the afternoon with him between her thighs, his hard back teasing her breasts each time she bounced against it? Or did she want to sit with her back against him, with the evidence of his arousal brushing against her? In a strangled voice she said, "We could walk."

"That's our wisest choice," he said with a wink that made the conversation feel less mortifying. It was as if they were on the same team, fighting the same weakness. He was also leaving the decision up to her which gave her confidence. Maybe the situation wasn't completely out of control.

"I'm not sorry I met you," she said softly.

He put out his hand for her to take and gave her a cocky smile. "I know."

JOSIE LED GABE to a large koi pond behind the house. Although many areas of the property were in disrepair, the pond was clear and well-maintained with fish well over a foot long. She threw in a handful of pellets and looked excited at each one that came to eat. "His name is Cow. Not just because he's black and white, but also because he eats more than any of them. Most of them eat their fill and stop. He'll eat as much as I feed them. That's Mr. Macho. He muscles his way through them. He's usually the first to check out something new and the last to leave. The orange one is Pumpkin. I almost named her hussy because a lot of the smaller koi look like her."

Gabe laughed. "They all look the same to me. Are you sure that's even a female?"

Her chin rose and she challenged, "Of course."

Remembering her joke about her dolls, he waited for her to smile and admit she couldn't either. When she didn't, he peered at the fish again and tried to look serious. "What are you basing your guess on? Depth of voice? Ability to drive?"

Her hands went to her hips. "First, if you're observant to details, classifying them is simple enough. The fins are slightly different. The body of the male tends to be leaner. Second, I've seen you drive so I'd be careful about using that to determine sex."

Slam. Hilarious. Gabe laughed and pulled her into his arms. "Question my manhood and I'll have to prove it to you."

Laughter mirrored in her eyes. "By listing football stats?"

He settled her pelvis against his. "My evidence is more concrete." He kissed her deeply until they were both shaking with need. "Damn, show me somewhere else before I start stripping us both right here." Desire raged in her eyes, and she looked as tempted as he was. She shook her head slightly and he groaned. He'd asked her to trust him, and he was determined to prove she could.

Their breathing slowly returned to normal and she asked, "Do you remember your tree house?"

"Vaguely, maybe." He couldn't think straight, never mind recall something he hadn't seen in over twenty years.

She stepped back but took his hand. "I found it during a walk one evening and fell in love with it. You really need to see it."

Right then, he would have followed her anywhere. As they walked down a wooded path to the tree house his father had built, memories flooded back. He'd always thought he liked independent women, but Josie took it to a new level. She had her vulnerable moments, but she was also confident and smart enough that he could imagine letting her take the lead now and then.

The tree house was in a state of disrepair with rotted boards and peeling paint, but his initials as well as those of all of his brothers were still visible. *Something I wouldn't have cared about last week.* Family was nice, but growing his business and accruing wealth was his focus. His older brother, James, was the same and he'd hit the billionaire status.

Nothing had mattered more than joining James there. Gabe hadn't seen value in anything from his past. *Always the future. Have I been wrong?*

For the first time, he not only missed his parents, but he missed his brothers. *Ridiculous, because I can see them whenever I want.*

But when was the last time I picked up the phone to call them? I'm losing them, not to death, but due to my own fault. A profound sadness settled over him. He hadn't expected to feel that way. Honestly, he hadn't expected visiting the ranch to be an emotional experience at all.

His father's death had brought his own mortality to the forefront. It's easy to imagine you'll live forever when your parents are alive, but when they're gone . . . you realize your generation is next.

What will I leave behind?

He'd never wanted to be encumbered with a wife and children, but the thought of dying without either wasn't what he wanted.

"Your father made this himself, didn't he? He didn't hire it out."

"You're right," Gabe said in surprise.

She smiled and ran a hand over the remaining slats of the wooden ladder. "I knew it was made with love. Your mother helped him design it."

"Why do you say that?"

"Because it has curtains."

"I never noticed them." But there they were . . . the tattered remains of them anyway. "I bet you're right."

She touched his carved initials. "Why did you decide not to keep the ranch?"

Gabe leaned a shoulder against the tree and looked down at her. "My father included an occupancy clause. I'd have to stay here for a month. There's too much going on at work for it to be worth it."

"How do your brothers feel about you not keeping it?"

"It's really none of their business. Dad gave something to each of us. I'm not getting involved in what they do with what they inherited. They know better than to try to tell me what to do with mine." She held his eyes long enough that he eventually confessed, "My mother's sister is the reason I'm here this weekend. She's hoping I keep it."

With her hands behind her, she rested her back on the tree beside his arm. "But you don't want to."

He bent so his face hovered above hers and growled, "Even if I wanted to keep it, it doesn't make sense to."

She licked her bottom lip. "I couldn't let it go. Not with everything that's here."

He bent closer. "I've gotten as far as I have by staying focused and keeping my life uncluttered."

"That'll make a depressing epitaph."

"Really? What will yours say?"

A corner of her mouth twitched with a hint of a

smile. "It all went to hell, but she meant well."

He chuckled.

She smiled.

He pivoted to stand in front of her and placed a hand on the tree beside her head. Even though she was smiling, there'd been a twinge of sadness in her voice. "Are things that bad?"

She touched his cheek gently. "Yes, but not when I'm with you."

Their connection shook him. He wanted her, but it was more than that. Refusing to overthink it, he groaned and claimed her mouth with his.

Chapter Eight

THREE MONTHS OF being utterly alone. Six months on the run. Years since a man's touch had brought her release. She didn't want to say no anymore. Not with Gabe. He deepened their kiss. There was no more thinking, only an urgency to experience *him*. She ran her hands up his flat stomach, across his chest, and encircled his neck. Arching brought her breasts fully against him, and she sighed at the pleasure that rocked through her.

He kissed his way across her cheek and neck. "God, you taste so good."

She licked her lips. "So do you."

With the sure moves of an experienced man, he lifted her shirt over her head between kisses, keeping her too mesmerized to protest. Her bra followed it to the ground. He cupped her breasts and they warmed beneath his adoring gaze. "So perfect."

She would have protested that she wasn't, but the ability to speak disappeared when his mouth closed over her nipple. "Oh, Gabe."

He paused just long enough to say, "I love the way you say my name."

"Gabe," she said again, breathlessly as she dug her hands into the back of his hair. His tongue was magic. She couldn't get enough of it. When he moved his attention to her other breast, she sought his manhood. Fully aroused, it easily filled her hand. She stroked it, loving the size of him.

He groaned and kissed his way back to her mouth. She took his tongue in, circling it with hers. His hands caressed her breasts, gently at first and then with skilled firmness that fueled the flame inside her.

She wanted more of him and began to frantically unbutton his shirt. Her fingers fumbled in their haste. Without breaking their kiss, he helped her finish and dropped his shirt onto the grass. Her hands went to the clasp of his khakis, and he covered her hand with his. "Are you sure?" he asked raggedly.

If she wasn't before, his question made up her mind. One night with a man like him was worth the heartache she'd feel the next day. "Shut up and kiss me," she said, intending it as a joke, but it came out as a desperate request.

He complied eagerly, unfastened her jeans, and slid them down along with her panties. "Gorgeous."

She felt beautiful in that moment. Beautiful and sexy. Young and free. Yesterday didn't matter. She wasn't thinking about tomorrow. There was only Gabe and the pleasure his mouth and hands brought everywhere they caressed.

She slid his pants down, loving how his shaft jutted

against her eagerly. He stepped back long enough to spread his shirt out on the grass beneath the tree house. She guessed his intention and lay across it. He sank to all fours between her legs. "I want to hear you say my name as you come, and you will. And you'll call it out when you're begging me to take you."

Josephine would have made a joke about his level of confidence, but when his tongue found her clit there was nothing funny about the pleasure that ripped through her. This was no fumbling boy. His tongue danced over her, dipped within her, brought her exactly where he'd promised to take her.

She cried out his name when she came and grasped his shoulders desperately. The waves of heat spreading through her weren't enough. She wanted him, needed him inside her. He reached for his pants and the short time it took for him to sheath himself in a condom felt like an eternity.

The wait proved worthy. He positioned himself between her legs, held his weight with one hand while using his other to lift one of her legs to his chest. His first thrust was gentle. His second was deeper. Each one that followed was faster and more forceful until she was writhing beneath him, meeting each thrust eagerly and begging him not to stop. There was no rush to this claiming, but she wasn't sure it could be called lovemaking. It was rough, primal. She'd never lost control during sex, but her previous experiences paled in comparison. Some part of her knew she was digging her nails into his back, but she didn't care. Waves of pleasure rocked through her again and this time he was right there with her, calling out . . .

Josie.

Because that's who he thinks I am.

A tear slid down her cheek. He kissed it away then groaned as he came. "Holy shit," he said. He took a moment to remove his condom then pulled her to his chest. "Holy shit that was good."

She rested her head on his chest and closed her eyes.

"Josie. Are you okay?"

She shook her head and kept her eyes closed.

"Look at me," he urged.

She covered her mouth with her hand, and tears that she fought to hold back spilled over. "I can't. I can't do this."

He hugged her. "Josie."

That only brought more tears. She opened her eyes but couldn't raise them to his. "Stop. Stop saying my name. Stop being so nice to me. Stop kissing me. Just stop."

He sat up and gave her a light shake. "You wanted me as much as I wanted you."

"I did," she said and pulled away from him, reaching for her bra and shirt, "but I didn't know I would feel this way."

"What way? Talk to me."

She shook her head again and continued dressing. There was no way to tell him without telling him everything. How could she explain that she'd thought being with him would make her feel less lonely, but hearing him call her the wrong name drove home how alone she actually was? He'd had sex with the woman he thought she was. *Not me.*

And instead of feeling better, she felt like she'd lost another piece of herself. She grabbed her shoes and started to walk away.

He pulled on his pants, chased after her and pulled her to a halt by her arm. His voice was tortured and deep. "If I hurt you—"

"You didn't."

"Someone did."

She looked into his concerned eyes and imagined what he'd say if she tried to explain. Would he believe any part of it?

And how would she begin to tell him?

Oh, sorry about the tears. I do that every time I lie about who I am to a man and then sleep with him. It's silly really. Why the lie? Nothing too big. Just a small misunderstanding involving a breached government contract, a company that may or may not want me dead, and the fact that I have enough possibly explosive material hidden in the back of the main garage to permanently put myself on a terrorist watch list. Besides that, really, there's not much going on.

He gripped her upper arms. "How can I help you if you won't talk to me?"

"Leave," she said quietly.

His hands tightened on her. "What?"

"I don't want to have dinner with you tonight. I want you to go. Please. Go tonight. Go now."

He dropped his hands. "Is that really what you want?"

She hugged her arms around herself. "Yes."

"I didn't mean to hurt you. I hate that I did." His face was tight and pale.

"You did nothing wrong. It's my problem. Not yours."

He pocketed his hands and hovered. "Do you need anything? I could find someone for you to talk to. It doesn't have to be me."

Tears welled again in her eyes. "I'm fine. I would leave if I could, but I can't so—"

"I'll walk you back."

She nodded and waited while he gathered up his things and put his shoes on. She'd never felt more lost or confused than when she left him on the steps of the guest house. After closing the door behind her she sank to the floor and hugged her knees to her chest.

I took something beautiful and made it ugly.

Gabe thinks he took advantage of a woman who has been abused.

I'd be afraid this will land me in hell, but I'm already there.

ONCE AGAIN IN a suit and tie, Gabe repacked his luggage as guilt crushed down on him. He hadn't lived a perfect life. Yes, there were things he'd done he wasn't proud of, but nothing like this. He'd never sunk so low that he couldn't look himself in the mirror. He felt physically sick that he'd allowed lust to overpower his sense of decency.

Josie had trusted him. She'd told him she wasn't ready for more. All the signs had been there that she needed time and patience. *But I plowed ahead because I couldn't keep my hands off her.*

Gabe was normally good at damage control, at least when it came to business. He could spin almost anything into a win, but there was no winning in this situation.

I hurt her.

A few days ago he would have said he was a good man. Maybe not one who remembered someone's birthday or brought soup to the sick, but he'd always fought a clean fight. Women had come and gone in his life, but he liked to think he'd always left them in as good or better a place than he found them. People envied Gabe, they didn't hate him.

They would if they'd seen Josie's tears. I did that. I should have made sure she was safe. I should have realized that a woman who pulls a gun on a stranger needs protection more than she needs a lover.

He approached his car then grimaced at the ding on the door. He shook his head in self-deprecation. *Yesterday, I thought a marred paint job was a big deal. Now I wish that were the only damage I'd done this weekend.*

Before getting into his car he walked over and placed a folded piece of paper in the door of the guest house. He almost knocked, but she'd asked him to go. *If I see her, I'll want to hold her until I know she's okay. But that's not what she wants.*

He sat in his car for a few minutes waiting for her to open the door of the house, but she didn't. Eventually he revved the engine and peeled out, not caring what damage the gravel did to the car as it flew up in his wake.

Because he couldn't bear the silence of the ride, Gabe called Hunter.

"Hey, I'm driving back from the ranch," Gabe said slowly.

"Aunt Claire told me you'd headed down there. I thought you were staying until tomorrow."

"I was."

"Still letting it go, I bet. I told her a weekend wouldn't make a difference. The tax write-off idea was genius. You always did know how to work the system."

"So you don't actually care if I keep it." It wasn't a question.

"Are you asking for my opinion?" Hunter sounded surprised.

"Yes. I would need to delay the occupancy part while I organized my office as well as figured out a few things, but I'm considering keeping it. I rode down to the canyon, and it wasn't what I expected."

"Wait, you rode down to the canyon on what?"

"An ATV I found in the garage."

"You weren't afraid it would wrinkle your suit?" Hunter teased although not in a mean fashion.

"I have other clothes." *Now.* "Being at the ranch brought back a lot of memories. It actually made me miss Dad. Imagine that."

Hunter whistled. "Are you drunk?"

Am I normally that much of a jackass that I'd have to be drunk to say I miss someone? "No, just thinking. A few years from now some of us will have families. The ranch was a good place for us when we were children. It might be good to keep it for the next generation."

"Are you *pregnant*?" Hunter asked with a laugh.

"I don't know why I thought talking to you would help."

"Sorry," Hunter said in a more serious tone. "I'm just not used to you coming to me for advice. Visiting the ranch sounds like it really affected you. If so, you should keep it."

"I couldn't understand why Dad would leave it to me, but you and I are old enough to remember what it was like to be there when Mom was alive. We were all different then."

"Because we were *kids*."

"Not just that. We were close, and it felt like we always would be."

"Shit, Gabe, are you okay?"

"I'll be back in my office by tonight. Work will improve my mood. It always does."

"Let's get together soon for a drink."

"Sounds good."

"Call me if you need me, Gabe. I'm serious."

"I'm fine, Hunter. Keep out of trouble."

"Now that is something I can't promise," Hunter answered with a chuckle and hung up.

Gabe decided work was the perfect salve. He listened to emails as he drove and dictated his response to several of them. Some would have to wait until he spoke to his team. Others required information that was on his computer.

My laptop.

Shit.

I left it at the ranch.

A glance down at the GPS revealed he was halfway to his apartment. He pulled over at the first rest stop to confirm that he had indeed forgotten to pack his laptop. *Shit.* Returning for it the next week wasn't an option; he had too many confidential files linked to it and too much work in progress on his desktop.

He could send someone else for it, but that seemed ridiculous. Although it would be a real pain in the ass, it made more sense to turn around and add a few hours to the trip. It didn't matter what time he got in. There was no chance he'd be able to sleep anyway. *And there's no one waiting for me there.*

I'll drive back to the ranch, grab the laptop, and go. It doesn't have to be more than that.

Unless Josie comes out when I return.

She might after she reads my note.

Chapter Nine

THERE WASN'T TIME to feel sorry for herself or sorry in general. As soon as Gabe was down the driveway, Josie called for the moving truck. Thankfully it was available. She arranged to be picked up and taken to the rental office, then she would drive herself back to the ranch. She'd leave behind the older car she'd bought for a few hundred dollars.

She quickly darkened her hair to jet black and chose equally dark contact lenses. To go along with the new identity, she put on a conservative flowered dress. She had enough cash to stay at a hotel for a short time, which would give her time to find a new place.

Julie. That sounds like a nice name.

A couple hours later, she loaded the last of the boxes into the back of the truck and was thankful the sun had set. The air had cooled and felt good on her warm cheeks. She wiped sweat from her forehead and sat on the steps of the guest house. All that was left to load was the bike and she would be done.

She pulled Gabe's note out of her back pocket and held it on her lap.

I have to read it.

I don't want to, but how can I not?

There's nothing he could have written that would make me feel better. On the other hand, I can't imagine I could feel worse than I do.

I didn't have to let him leave thinking he'd hurt me. Even if I couldn't tell him the truth, I could have made up another lie—one that would have made him hate me instead of himself.

She closed her eyes briefly then, after taking a fortifying breath, opened them along with the note.

Josie,

I don't have the words to express how sorry I am. You trusted me, and I didn't honor your trust or you the way I should have. I could tell you that I've never wanted a woman as desperately as I wanted you, but that would sound like I'm trying to excuse my actions. There is no excuse.

You don't have to tell me what you've been through, but please let me help you. I'll hold off sending my team to work on the house. I have to make a decision about the ranch soon, but I'll put it off as long as I can.

If you need a place to stay, I'll help you find one.

I never meant to hurt you. If you believe nothing else, believe that.

You deserve better than I brought this weekend, and I don't expect you to forgive me,

but I hope that you'll let me make things easier for you.

You don't have to face your demons alone,
Gabe

Josephine hugged the note to her chest and gave in to the tears she'd been holding back. *How do I make this right?*

How did trying to do something good bring me here?

She went into the house and then the office. She sat at the desk and turned the note over. Maybe she couldn't fix the rest of the situation she was in, but she could fix this.

Gabe,

You will never know how sorry I am that I let you leave still believing you'd hurt me. My tears were not because of you. No one hurt me, not the way you think. You didn't break my trust; I violated yours.

Telling you would involve you in a legal mess and potentially put you in danger. If anyone asks, I was gone before you got here. It'll be better for you if everyone believes that.

I lied to you about many things, but this is the truth: I wanted what we did. I didn't want to spend the rest of my life regretting that I missed my chance to be with you. I cried because my lies kept it from being what it should have been.

Please don't be sorry.

I'm sorry.

And don't worry when you see that I'm gone. I'll land on my feet. I always do.

You are a wonderful man. I wish we had met when I could have told you my real name.

Josephine

She propped the note against the lamp on the desk and rose to her feet. It was only then that she noticed a laptop on the shelf beside it. It didn't look like Frank's. It was too new to be one that had been left behind years ago.

Oh, no.

Gabe's. If he realizes he left it here . . .

She rushed to the hidden lab in the main garage where the bike was still stored. She pushed it out onto the driveway to where she'd parked the truck. She was tying it against one side of the interior when she heard the crunch of tires on gravel.

No. No. No.

If I'm fast, I can pull out before he realizes what I'm doing. Yes, his car can outrun this heap, but that would mean he'd have to chase me and he won't. He feels too badly to do that.

It was only then that Josephine remembered her dress didn't have pockets. The keys to the truck were with her purse—in the guest house.

I'm screwed.

No. Don't panic. He's back for his laptop, not me. I just need to play it cool long enough for him to go into the house to get it. That'll give me time to get the keys and leave before he realizes what I'm doing. She stepped out of the back of the truck and was in the process of pulling the door down when Gabe appeared at the bottom of the truck ramp.

"Josie?" He looked her over from head to toe then looked her over again. "Your hair is black."

Shit. Stay calm. She forced a smile. "I wanted a change."

"And your eyes—you have blue eyes, but they're black now." She could see him processing what that meant and cringed at what she knew was coming. "They were brown when you first met me, weren't they?"

"Yes."

He frowned and looked from her to the moving truck to her again. "You're leaving tonight?"

She clasped her hands in front of her. "It's for the best."

"Did you find my note?" he asked in a tight voice.

"I did. I wrote you one on the back of it and left it on the desk."

His expression darkened. "I meant every word. I can't tell you—"

"I can't talk about it now, but read my note." Trying to distract him from the truck, she walked down the ramp. "When I was in the office in the main house, I saw your laptop. You should go get it before you forget it again."

He stepped closer and touched her cheek tenderly. "I

don't care about that. Where are you going?"

She laid her hand over his and removed it from her face. "I have friends." *One more lie for the road, but at least this one is to make him feel better.*

"You don't have to leave."

"I do." *All you have to do is walk away long enough so I can grab my keys.* She didn't allow herself the luxury of emotions. She knew if she did, she would crack and tell him everything.

Which would be yet another selfish decision.

"Did I see a motorcycle in the truck?"

"What?"

"A black motorcycle. You have one in your truck, but I don't remember seeing one on the ranch."

"It's dark. You must have seen a table and thought it was a bike." A hundred possible lies might have appeased him. She'd uttered the only one that wouldn't, and she knew it as soon as it was past her lips.

"Really?" he said as he walked up the ramp. "Mind if I take a peek at the table that looks so much like a motorcycle?" He rolled the back door of the truck up. When he turned back to her, his expression was dark.

IT WAS A slow downshift from guilt to suspicion, but Gabe had never been the most trusting of souls. He didn't believe in fate or most people, which was why he had full-time private investigators on his payroll. Business and personal relationships worked out better when there were no secrets. He'd broken his pattern by sleeping with Josie before knowing more about her.

His gut told him he'd let that beautiful face of hers lead him up a tree with brittle branches and the tumble down might be a painful one. Women dyed their hair. It might mean nothing. Some used color contacts as an enhancement. Again, not a big deal.

Then why lie about it? Vanity? It didn't fit what he knew about her.

But what do I really know?

I should have called Frank. She said he knows she's here, but does he? She could be anyone.

A thief even—one trying to leave with a truckload of my family's things. Or Frank's.

And I slept with her.

Dammit, what the hell was I thinking?

He remembered how upset she'd been right after they'd had sex. Her tears had been real.

Or she'd wanted him to think they were.

Why?

None of it made sense. He hadn't liked thinking he'd hurt her, but he didn't like the alternative any better. Had she played him?

If so, why sleep with me?

Because it put me right where she wanted me? On the defensive? Feeling so guilty that I wouldn't ask questions?

"Does the bike even belong to you?"

Her mouth opened and shut like a fish trying to breath before she said, "Yes."

He walked down the ramp and planted himself directly in front of her. "I want to believe you."

She looked him in the eye. "You can. It is mine."

A confusing kaleidoscope of emotions swirled within him. If everything was a lie it meant he hadn't hurt her, which would be a relief. On the other hand, he didn't want to think she was capable of that kind of deception. She might still be the woman he thought she was. Did she change her hair color to hide from a man? "Are you hiding from someone?" His next thought wasn't as kind. "The police?"

She looked away. "Of course not."

Was that guilt or shame? He couldn't tell. He turned his attention back to something concrete that might provide him with actual answers. "What's in the boxes?"

Her eyes flew to his again. "Just my things."

He tested her by watching her expression closely while he said, "You understand I have to check that you're being honest. My father kept some collectibles here. Things that would be impossible to replace." It wasn't true, but she didn't know that.

All color drained from her face. "I'm not a thief."

He walked over to one of the boxes and lifted the lid, continuing to watch her reaction while he did. When he looked down at the contents finally, he saw only hair brushes and a few towels and felt like a complete idiot. He replaced the cover, ran a hand through his hair, and his shoulders sagged as another wave of remorse swept over him. "I'm sorry. You must think I'm the biggest asshole. I know you're not a thief."

She swallowed visibly. "Thank you."

He laughed without humor. "When I hoped to have another chance to talk to you this weekend, this wasn't how I imagined it going."

"I understand. You don't know me and how I'm leaving looks damning, but I didn't think it was right if I stayed." She cleared her throat nervously. "Don't feel badly about anything that happened between us. I was upset, but not because you did anything wrong. You did everything right. I'm the one who should be sorry."

Her words lifted the weight that had sat heavily on him since he'd left her. A brief giddiness filled him. *I didn't hurt her.* He was filled with a crazy desire to whoop and swing her around. Things were not as bad as he'd thought they were. That meant . . . "Is there any way we could start over? I'll even let you pull the gun on me again if you want. That was hot." Gabe replayed his own words in his head and groaned. "I need you to speak with people who know me. They'll tell you I am not usually a bumbling idiot."

"You're not an idiot," she said softly.

He leaned in. It was impossible to stand so close to her and not remember the taste of her, to not crave her. He told himself that this thinking led to them rolling around on his shirt beneath the tree house. Which had been a bad decision. But if that were true, why was she standing there looking like she wanted him again? "I feel like one whenever I'm with you. I know what you said earlier. I understand that you don't want this, but God, I want to kiss you. And despite everything that happened today, I think you want me to. Tell me I'm wrong. Or right."

She licked her lips but she neither agreed nor denied his claim. "I—you—" She stopped and shook her head. "I don't know what to say."

He ran his thumb lightly across her parted lips. "All I want is the truth."

Chapter Ten

*I*T SHOULDN'T BE *this hard. I should be able to tell him whatever he wants to hear and leave knowing that it was the best choice for both of us.*

What am I hoping for? That he believes me? What then? Does he help me hide? Wait until I clear my father's name? What if I don't? What happens then? Would a man like him want the daughter of a man accused of fraud?

And worse, much worse, what if I tell him, and he gets hurt trying to help me? I'll then be responsible for the death of two men. Would I be able to live with that?

I don't want to lie to him anymore.

"The truth is I wasn't expecting anyone like you to come into my life. That's why you're getting mixed signals. I like you, but I'm not ready to be with anyone."

Gabe's hand dropped to his side. "I see."

"I'm sorry."

He frowned and pocketed his hands. "No, I appreciate your candor." His tone was formal and Josephine wondered if that was his defense. "I'm sorry, too." He looked her over slowly. "I'm curious. Why change your hair and eye color? Why the fake tattoo?"

She almost said she liked variety, but being honest

with him made her feel like she could breathe again. "It makes my life easier."

"I don't understand."

"I know."

He looked back into the truck. "That's a unique bike."

"My dad and I made it."

He nodded. "After how you described him, I can imagine the two of you working on it together."

Just then the clasp that she'd used to secure the bike let go, and the bike crashed onto its side, taking down a pile of boxes with it. The contents of some spilled onto the floor of the truck. Unfortunately, one of those boxes held her cash and the fake driver's licenses she'd created for herself when she'd left the East Coast. Motels required IDs, and she'd wanted to cover her tracks well so she'd made several with different ages and names.

Before Josephine could stop him, Gabe rushed into the truck to right her bike. She knew the moment he saw the IDs because he froze. In painful slow motion, he set the bike onto its stand and began picking up the licenses. He looked as angry as he'd once looked concerned. "Who the hell are you?"

Time for honesty was over. Josephine bolted toward the guest house. He followed in quick pursuit, closing the distance between them with much more speed than she'd anticipated. She was in the process of opening the door to the guest house when he slammed it shut and spun her around.

She considered kneeing him but hesitated and lost the advantage when he guessed her intent. *And this is why you don't sleep with someone you may have to run from. I can't hurt him.*

His hand bit into her arm, and she amended her thoughts.

Much. She tried to knock his hand off and used a self-defense trick she'd been taught to free herself. It didn't work. His hold on her tightened.

Her temper rose. "Let go of my arm."

"Answer my question."

GABE HAD NEVER hurt a woman, but he wanted to throttle her. She'd made a fool of him again and again. Remembering how he'd beaten himself up over upsetting her flamed his anger. Whatever game she was playing would end right then and there. "You can tell me or the police, but you're not going anywhere until I know who you are and what the hell you're doing here."

Her eyes rounded with panic. "Don't call the police."

"Then start talking, although depending on what I hear I may call them anyway."

The pleading look she gave him might have worked earlier, but not anymore. "I'm not a criminal if that's what you're thinking."

"You've said that before, but you'll have to excuse me for not believing you."

Her bottom lip jutted out. "Why ask me anything if you're not going to believe what I say?"

"I'll believe your name because I can check it. What is it?" He threw the IDs at her feet. "Not any of these. The real one."

She pressed her lips together, seeming to weigh her options.

In hostile negotiations the winner was the one who had the least to lose. Gabe nodded at the truck. "How much is what you have in the truck worth to you? It means nothing to me. A match and some gasoline would get rid of half of my problem."

"You wouldn't. It's a rental."

He laughed at that. "Not under my name."

She glared at him. "Try it and you'll kill us both. There are enough volatile chemicals in the truck to flatten everything in a three-hundred-foot radius."

"Now that sounds like something the police would be interested in."

Stubborn grit shone in her eyes. "It may not look like it, but I do care about you. That's why I don't want you involved in this."

He shook his head. *Try again, babe. I'm not swallowing that one.*

With an audible sigh of frustration, she said, "You win. I'll tell you who I am, but promise me you'll hear me out before you decide what to do."

"You're not in the position to ask me for anything." He turned and used his phone to take a photo of the truck then snapped a photo of her. He sent both to his security team along with a dictated request for them to check in with him in thirty minutes. If he didn't answer his phone they were to call the police and give them her photo.

"What are you doing?" she asked.

"I'm making sure you won't make it far if you clock me in the head with something."

"Who did you send my photo to?"

"My security team. Call it insurance. Plus, it'll help confirm your identity. Now, what's your name?"

"Josephine Ashby." Her shoulders slumped a bit as she said it.

Ashby. The name was familiar, but he couldn't place why. He sent it to his team and told them he wanted as much as they could find, and he wanted it immediately. "What was your father's name? Assuming you actually were close to him."

"Roy Ashby. Everything I said about him was true. He was a good man with a big dream that got ahead of him."

A moment or so after sending both names to his team, his phone binged with a photo of her as a blonde standing beside an older man. He confirmed that the woman in the photo was the one he wanted information on, along with anything they could uncover about her father. Message after message came in with links to articles about her father. One was a press release from Raymean Industries. He read it over. It described how her father had died, trying to dispose of evidence that would have proven him guilty of fraud. Raymean was unable to fulfill a large government contract because Ashby had lied about his ability to produce the bike, StealthOff. He finished the article while holding Josie—Josephine—by the arm. "If your father was the one who defrauded Raymean, why are you in hiding? Do you have the money they say he embezzled?"

She tugged at her arm. "My father didn't embezzle from anyone. I'll tell you everything, but not while you're manhandling me."

He almost loosened his hold but thought better of it. She was feisty and seemed to know a fair share of self-defense moves. "You'll tell me first, and then I'll consider releasing you."

"And if you don't like what you hear? What are you going to do? Tie me up?" she volleyed back.

"If I have to." An image of her spread eagle, tied to his bed, sent his blood rushing downward. The problem with interrogating her was that she had a dangerous ability to turn him on and his brain off. If she licked those pouty lips again he might well forget why he was holding her and take her right there on the steps. It didn't help that she was looking at him with the same hunger he was fighting off.

"Raymean killed my father."

"Why would they? That doesn't make sense. They say he took their money with no intention of producing a product. They'd want him alive so they could prosecute him."

"The only money he took from Raymean was what

he needed for the lab. I don't know what happened to the money they're talking about."

"And what money did *you* take?" He didn't know how much money she had stashed in those boxes, but the amount he'd seen fall onto the floor of the truck was in large bills.

"I emptied my savings when I ran."

"Your father died trying to steal the evidence. You're hiding out on the other side of the country. Your actions speak for themselves. I don't believe your story."

"Do you believe *this*?" She kicked his shin then— hard. It was unexpected and painful.

He grabbed her other arm and held her still. "What the hell is wrong with you?"

"What the hell is wrong with *me?* Maybe just that my father was killed and no one will pull their heads out of their asses long enough to question Raymean's lies. My father would never have ridden that bike. We knew it was dangerous. It was a prop. A dummy bike we kept at Raymean while we worked on the real one."

"The one in the truck." She'd said she'd built it with her father.

With her chest heaving, she ground out, "Yes. When it came to inventing things, my father was good with the big picture. He'd come up with the idea, and I'd find a way to make it possible. As soon as we had a working alternative power cell, we were going to swap the bikes out. Raymean was going to get their product." Her eyes filled with tears. "They didn't have to kill him. They would have gotten what they wanted."

He thought about how she'd periodically spoke in geek-ese and then brushed it off. *Science channel, my ass. I knew she was brilliant.* His grip on her loosened. "Why doesn't the article say anything about you if you were working with him?"

"No one knew. My father and I shared whatever we made, but it was his name on all the projects."

Gabe tried to imagine anyone happily remaining in the shadows while their work was being claimed by someone else. "How do I know you didn't kill your father because you felt he was stealing your ideas?"

She blinked quickly a few times, then answered. "If I were a killer I would have shot you when you arrived. No one besides Frank knows I'm here. It would have been easier than waiting for you to leave and hoping you didn't find the bike."

Looking back at their time together through that lens twisted Gabe's emotions. He'd genuinely liked her, but everything he thought he knew about her was a lie. *Except that she was smart.* She wanted him to believe she and her father were innocent, but how could he believe anything she said? Her version of how her father had died didn't make sense. A company as big as Raymean wouldn't kill someone, and if they did, they wouldn't do it in a high-profile lab explosion that made them look bad. "Why are you hiding if you've done nothing wrong?"

She took a deep breath. "After they killed him, they

came looking for me. Maybe they thought I had his designs. I don't know. No one knew about the second bike or that I was helping him. My father wouldn't have said anything about it. We'd worked on many projects together, and he'd never said a word."

"And you were okay with that? Never getting any recognition?"

Her gaze was steady. "I had my father. *That's* all that mattered. I would have done anything to keep him safe. Anything." She shook beneath Gabe's hold. "I thought when he retired from the Army he would be safe. I thought I knew best. It's my fault he's dead."

Gabe could see the pain in her eyes. Why would she believe she was responsible when she blamed Raymean? And what exactly was the equipment she was attempting to steal away? Why the aliases? "How did you end up here? How do you know Frank?"

"He was an inventor like my father." She referenced the ranch around them. "He took the job as caretaker because he wanted a place where he could tinker unencumbered without fearing people would steal his ideas."

Gabe remembered what he'd drawn in the ledger. "What was he working on before he left? The big metal tub." When she looked surprised, he added, "He left papers behind in my father's office. It looked like a bomb design."

She shook her head. "Frank? His last invention was a horizontal toaster that slid bread out onto a plate when it was done. He was working on a clothing hamper that could wash and then dry a person's clothing. Please don't tell anyone. He thinks it'll be huge."

Her last words were uttered in a whisper with a small smile that made him want to hug her. She'd made a fool of him over and over again, and he hated the part of himself that wanted to believe her. The idea of holding her quickly brought on a slew of other things he'd love to do to her. *Other women never made me this stupid. No wonder we're slow to evolve as a species. She's weaving a tale of corporate corruption and all I can think about is how she'd whisper my name in wonder if I teased her nipples with my teeth.* After a few long moments, he realized she was waiting for a response from him. *I'm a jackass. Focus. I can't stand here holding on to her forever.*

His phone beeped. He called his team and told them he was fine but to keep digging for more on her and her father. He wanted to know the name of her childhood pets. Everything. "You're not leaving tonight."

"Why would I stay? And before you say because you won't let me go, I need to warn you that tying me up won't be as easy as you think."

He didn't doubt that claim at all. Nothing about her was easy, and that was part of what he found exciting. "I won't have to restrain you." He let her go. "You'll stay on your own volition."

She took a step back, looking like she was gauging if she could make it inside the house before him. "And why would I do that?"

He confidently pocketed his hands. Unlike her, he had nothing to lose. "Run and I'll tell the police everything. There'll be nowhere you can hide after that."

She searched his face. "But you won't tell them if I stay?" A blush spread up her neck and across her cheeks. "If you think I'll sleep with you in exchange for your silence—"

"Whether or not you'd sleep with me has already been answered, but that's not what I'm offering you." Yes, not calling the police allowed for the possibility that he'd end up locked in the trunk of his car wondering why the hell he'd let his dick take the lead in this decision. His gut told him it was worth the risk, and he was rarely wrong. Except the time he broke his arm. Hunter had convinced him that being deposited on top of a mountain and having to ski back to civilization was better than staying at a resort. And when Hunter had talked him into going shark fishing. *So, my instincts are fine; it's Hunter's that will get me killed.* "You want someone to believe you're innocent? Convince *me.*"

Then sleep with me again.

Or the reverse.

God, I hope she's not a criminal.

Chapter Eleven

G ABE LOOKED SO cocky Josephine half wished she were the type to knock someone out and disappear into the night. *Convince me.* The way he said it sounded a lot like he was asking for a repeat performance of their earlier romp.

Or is that wishful thinking?

I'm fighting for my life here. I should not be looking at him like a starving person who stumbled across a steak. There is absolutely nothing sexy about how I couldn't get away from him until he let me go.

It doesn't matter that he's so strong. So tall. And when he chased me it reminded me of every fantasy I've ever had about being taken by a marauding pirate.

He threated to turn me in if I leave.

What would he think if he knew how much I want to stay?

She chewed her bottom lip. *This is everything I didn't want. What happened to not wanting to involve him? Not putting him in harm's way?*

"I don't know what Raymean will do if they find me—or you, if you're associated with me." *He has to know there might be consequences.*

He frowned. "I have people I trust. We'll be safe."

His confidence reminded her of what her father had said just before he died, and panic welled within her. She felt like she might throw up. "Call the police. Tell them you found me here and have no idea what I'm doing on the property. I couldn't bear it if you get yourself killed, too."

His frown deepened. "No one is going to kill me."

She threw her hands up in the air. "They killed my father. They lied to cover it up. Why wouldn't they do the same to us? Do you think your tie collection and pretty smile is going to save us?"

His head snapped back. "Not that I need to prove myself to you, but real estate is a cut-throat business. You don't make it to the top by letting anyone intimidate you. I've tangled with everyone from senators to mob bosses, and I've won. I don't fight dirty, but I'll take down anyone who comes for me. Convince me they did what you say, and we'll tear Raymean apart from the inside out."

Wow.

A spark of hope lit within her. She might, just might, have someone on her side. That feeling was followed by a gnawing fear that things had gone from very bad to possibly catastrophic. If she allowed herself to care for Gabe, care for anyone, she was giving Raymean the chance to take someone else from her, either physically or with their lies. "Can your security team be trusted?"

"I wouldn't keep them if I questioned their loyalty.

Yes."

She swallowed her fear. She and her father had never thought security was necessary, and that hadn't ended well for them. "Then you should have a few of them here. Just in case."

He gave her a long, steady look then nodded.

"What do you know about stabilizing the discharge of magnesium-ion?" she asked.

He tapped the breast pocket of his jacket where he kept his phone. "What I can google tonight."

Convince him? How? "I can show you my notes, but they won't prove much if you don't know the issues with current power cells on stealth vehicles or the challenges I'm facing with the ones I'm hoping will replace them. I'm making progress, but it's a leap forward, a slide back, then nothing until another leap. Just because it doesn't work yet doesn't mean I'm not close."

"I'm a reasonably intelligent man. Explain it, and I'll get it."

"I can't reduce everything I've done down to a five-minute presentation."

"You don't have to." He took out his phone and sent off a text. "You have a month."

"A month?" Her jaw fell open. She'd been living day to day, not allowing herself to think long term. Too many questions descended upon her whenever she asked herself where this would lead. When she did stabilize the power cell, and she was confident she would, she'd have a tool to clear her father's name and face Raymean head-on. First she'd prove that the project they claimed was impossible had been very much possible. Then, somehow, she'd use that to find out what happened to him.

Although she'd never wavered in her resolve, she'd imagined vindicating her father alone. She didn't know if the possibility of having Gabe by her side made that fated day more or less scary.

"I just told my lawyer I'm keeping the ranch. That means for the next thirty-one days I live in Calabasas. I'll work from here and no one will question why. You can use that time to build a case for why anyone should believe you. That is, of course, if you're not still lying."

"I'm not."

"Then tell me which boxes you need moved into the main house tonight. We'll move the rest in tomorrow."

"I'm not staying in the main house."

He stepped closer, towering over her. "I don't trust you as far as I can throw you. I'm not letting you out of my sight until I make up my mind about you."

MAN, THAT'S HOT.

I know, I know. I can't help myself. Look at those eyes. After today, all of my fantasy pirates will have his hazel eyes. They'll all kiss the way Gabe Brannigan does and have hands that reduce me to mindless submission.

I should demand to stay in the guest house again, but— seriously? I don't want to be alone and afraid because I think every noise means Raymean found me.

"Fine," she said, hoping she sounded irritated with

him. "But only because you've left me no choice."

His smile was wickedly smug as if he knew exactly why she'd agreed.

LATER THAT NIGHT, Gabe rolled over in his bed and punched his pillow. Not every idea he had was a good one.

He thought he'd planned for everything. Two key members of his security team were on their way to the ranch. They'd been instructed to stop at his apartment and pack everything from the list he'd sent. He sent his office staff instructions for how to keep him in the loop while covering what he couldn't while he fulfilled the requirements of his father's will. Food was scheduled for delivery. He'd even called his aunt and told her he'd decided to keep the ranch but that working from there would have him so busy he'd appreciate if no one visited. She promised to spread the word.

The keys to his car as well as the rental were on his nightstand along with the batteries from both the old car she'd worked on and the truck. Her gun was locked in the safe in his father's office. Her bike was upstairs in the hallway outside their bedrooms. Not an easy feat, but one he was certain she couldn't undo without a substantial amount of noise.

He'd thought of everything—except how it would feel to sleep in the same house as Josephine and not be able to go to her. *That* was pure torture.

This has to be as difficult for her. If not, I'm some kind of sick pervert who is essentially holding a woman hostage.

He rolled over again and covered his face with his pillow. *A month is a very long time if this doesn't turn out well.*

It could have been the lateness of the hour, but he found some of the situation pathetically amusing. *Daddy, tell me the story again about how you met Mommy.*

Well, it all started when Daddy lost his business because he was caught harboring a criminal . . .

Why, Daddy? Why would you do something that stupid?

One day, son, you'll meet a woman who turns your brain to oatmeal and your dick to a pogo stick in your pants. The only thing that will feel worse than being with her will be the idea of never seeing her again.

Is that what this is?

He rolled over again. *I don't even want kids. What the hell is she doing to me?*

Chapter Twelve

JOSEPHINE WOKE IN a good mood. She smiled through her shower, something she hadn't realized until she caught her expression in the bathroom mirror. *It's just because I'm not tired for once.* Knowing Gabe was in the next room had made her feel safe enough that she'd slept deeper than she had since she'd lost her father. Six months of suppressed grief, fear of discovery, and brain-stretching research had left her feeling frayed. *Is it simply because Gabe is formidable that I feel . . . calm beneath his shelter?* Knowing his men would be there by morning had added an extra feeling of peace. *Odd.*

I'm not sure if he's my captor or my protector.

I wonder if he knows.

Gabe hadn't taken advantage of the fact that they'd been alone in the house, and she hadn't expected him to. He was a man of integrity. Her honesty track record was shaky, but his was solid. She knew he still wanted her. His hot gaze followed her, but that was perfectly fine because she was finding it equally impossible to concentrate on anything but him.

The uncertainty of the situation, though, had reset

their relationship. It wasn't as if they could pick up where they'd left off. Everything had changed. They needed to find their footing with each other again.

I keep thinking of him in terms of how he makes me feel instead of focusing on the reality of our situation. We barely know each other. He doesn't believe me now, and he may never. Where will that land us? Perhaps there will be no us . . . not that I ever believed it was possible.

Choosing the proper attire for the day proved harder than she'd anticipated. She normally didn't think much about what she wore, but every option sent a message. She didn't want to look like she was dressing to impress him, but she wanted to hold his attention. This time not because she needed to distract him.

Knowing he was as attracted to her as she was to him was a heady feeling she wasn't ready to destroy with a frumpy outfit. She finally decided on jean shorts, a simple T-shirt, and no contacts. The contrast of her jet black hair and her light blue eyes was striking, but still not her.

She followed the aroma of coffee to the kitchen. Several plates of food were set out on the table. Scrambled eggs. Pancakes. Bowls of cut fruit. "You were busy this morning." She thought about it and asked, "Or is this the chef again?"

He smiled, stood, and held out a chair for her. "Of course it's the chef. My cooking skills begin and end with making coffee."

"Mine, too." When she sat down, he hovered behind

her chair for a moment. She thought he was about to lean down and kiss her, but he straightened and took the seat across from her. She picked up her fork and stabbed an egg. "Do you think it's odd that we're having breakfast like we're friends?"

He'd been in the middle of taking a sip of coffee and lowered his mug to the table before answering. "I considered sliding a tray of food under your door, but the chef insisted on serving it here." His voice was so serious she almost missed the twinkle in his eyes.

She popped a bite of egg into her mouth and chewed while rolling her eyes. "You know you don't scare me. I slept like a baby last night."

"I slept like shit," he said grumpily.

She laughed, and he almost smiled.

"I read your note."

Josephine dropped her fork, then picked it up again, trying not to look as anxious to hear his response as she was. "And?"

"You didn't have to write anything to me. You could have simply left before I returned."

"I knew what you thought had happened between us, and I couldn't let you keep thinking that. I hated that I let you think it at all."

He studied her for several moments. "I can't decide if you are the most calculating person I've ever met or a good person stuck in an extraordinarily horrific situation."

She shot him a pained smile. "I don't blame you for

not believing me. My friends wanted to believe the worst of me and my father. It was an education in human nature. If something is printed in a newspaper or reported in the news, it has to be true. So many people have stopped thinking for themselves, they just gobble the news up as if it can't be tainted or scripted."

"What do you think your father was doing in the lab that night? Why would he have ridden the bike if he knew it was dangerous?"

She pushed the food around her plate. "I don't know. I've asked myself that same question every day since he died. He wouldn't have ridden it. He had no reason to."

"What will you do when you stabilize the discharge from the power cell?"

Her eyebrows rose. He acted as if he understood what she was doing, even though he was only repeating back to her what she'd explained to him the night before. Still, it gave her hope. "I haven't decided. Part of me wants to go public. Raymean said my father knew his idea would never work. I could prove that was a lie. On the other hand, a working design for StealthOff would be worth a significant amount to Raymean and its competitors. I could use it as leverage to buy the truth about what really happened to my father. The lab has security cameras, but there was no recording of that night. Gone. Someone has to know what was on that video."

"There was no mention of missing security footage."

"Exactly."

Gabe drank more of his coffee, and Josephine could see him mulling over what she'd told him. "No video. Either your father messed with their system—"

"Or it's a cover-up."

He shook his head in skepticism. "A cover-up that big wouldn't be easy. If Raymean wanted to get rid of your father, they had less public options. Death in a lab fire. That involves the police, the media. It's too risky to have been a plan."

Josephine sat back in her chair and pushed the rest of her food away. "I don't know why they did it, but they did, and I'll prove it."

His watched her intently. "If you're right, only someone of influence could make a problem that big go away."

"I don't care. What would you do if your father had died at the hands of someone else?"

"I'd go after them with everything I had."

"Then you understand why I didn't want to involve you. This is my problem. If you change your mind and decide not to be part of it, I'll understand. Finishing the bike is the easy part. Things might get ugly very fast after that."

He leaned forward, resting his elbows on the table and looking her in the eye. "You sound so damn convincing."

"Because I'm telling the truth."

"This time," he said with some irony.

"Yes. This time." He knew the reasons why she'd lied to him. She would try to prove to him that the power cell was near completion. Beyond that, it would be up to him to decide who to believe—*the news or me*.

"My men are here. If you leave now it will be without your bike or your things."

"I agreed to show you my research."

He simply held her gaze.

She sighed. "I won't run off." He opened his mouth to respond, but she waved a hand to silence him. "You don't trust me. I get it. But, tell me something, if I'm such a horrible person, why are you here with me? Why didn't you call the police? I don't understand why you're going to all this effort to find out the truth."

He sat back as he considered his answer. "I could say the truth has always been important to me."

"But?"

"But I wouldn't normally get involved in something like this."

"So, why this time?"

He placed his napkin on the table and stood. "I'm ready to see the research."

She walked around the table and planted herself in front of him. "No. Not until you answer me. Why are you still here?"

He searched her face and frowned. "Because I want you to be innocent and, if you are, I want to keep you safe."

Despite his gruff tone, his words were sincere and

sweet. They shot right through Josephine's defenses and exploded like fireworks in what remained of her fragmented heart. She smiled and wiped a stray tear from the corner of her eye. "Don't you dare get killed helping me."

He looked surprised by her request, then chuckled. *That smile. It might be my undoing. Endearing. Sexy.* "That's not in my plan."

Josephine turned and led the way out of the kitchen toward the office where her server and notes were still in boxes. "You have a plan? You're already better at this than I am."

GABE STOOD IN the doorway of his father's office while Josephine checked the contents of the boxes they'd placed there last night. She didn't appear to be attempting to hide anything.

"It's a waste of time to unpack everything in here. To really see what I was doing we need to put all of this back in my lab."

"You have one here?"

The look she gave him as much as asked, "Do I breathe air?" but her actual answer was less sarcastic. "I walled off a part of the main garage and built a hidden one there."

He waved a finger in the air. "No wonder I remembered it bigger."

"I know. I truly thought you were going to question why, but Frank did a fantastic job at recreating the far wall. It blends perfectly."

"You said Frank and your father were friends. I'm surprised he left you on your own."

Josephine knelt beside one of the boxes and reclosed the top of it. "You wouldn't if you knew Frank. He and my father used to live in the same neighborhood as children. Dad joined the Army at eighteen. Frank came out to California to make his fortune, but Dad said he didn't have the social skills to take advantage of the location. Frank isn't dangerous, but he's a little different. I'm not entirely sure it's not voices in his head that give him ideas for his inventions. He's brilliant, but he's also obsessive and reclusive." She smiled at a memory. "For fun I asked him why his clothing hamper could do everything except put the clothing on hangers. I joked that no one wants to come home to wrinkled clothing. He's been trying to design a robotic arm option since. If he figures it out, I'll be his first customer. I hate hanging clothes."

"You didn't tell him about your father."

"No. He wouldn't have been able to handle it. I told him Dad died in a lab fire. That's all he needed to know."

"Didn't he think it was odd that you wanted to hide out here and build a secret lab?"

She shook her head slowly. "No, to him that was completely normal."

It all made sense but Gabe wasn't sold yet. "How the hell does a man like that have a daughter?"

She shrugged. "Every pot has a lid? Dad said Frank was married for a short time. She wanted him to get a regular job. I don't know who left whom, but the marriage didn't last long. I feel sorry for him. He lives a very lonely life. I didn't know what lonely was until I came here. I was beginning to go stir crazy before you showed up. I thought I liked being alone but this is a whole new level of alone."

He thought back over their first meeting and rest of the weekend, seeing it very differently as the truth of what she must have been thinking at the time sunk in. "Did you agree to spend time with me because you wanted to or so I wouldn't look around the ranch?"

She chewed her bottom lip before answering. "Both."

He slammed his hand against the wall beside him with enough force that she jumped. He could have asked more questions, but for once, he wasn't sure he wanted the whole truth. He walked over, picked up a box and said, "We might as well get started. Your lab won't rebuild itself."

She looked as if she wanted to say something then decided against it. Instead she bent and also picked up a box. "Do you know anything about setting up computer servers?"

He employed people who did that kind of thing for him, but he wasn't about to admit that. He picked up a second box and said, "I'm sure I can figure it out."

Her lips twitched with a smile she was holding back. "If you'd like I can give you a few minutes to google it."

He strode out of the office instead of dropping the boxes and kissing her senseless like he wanted to. His rational side knew he shouldn't lower his guard, but that didn't change how good it felt to be with her. Josephine was a complex woman. She was as tough as she was sexy and as snarky as she was sweet. Every moment with her felt fresh, and he'd never met a woman who made him feel so alive.

They made several trips from the house to the garage and then from the truck to the garage. He had one of his men help with the move, but dismissed him while the boxes were still closed. He trusted him, but he kept his employees on a need-to-know basis. If they didn't need it, they didn't need to know it. His men knew who Josephine was and what she'd claimed had happened to her father, but they didn't need to know how close she was or wasn't to finding a solution.

Josephine worked on her lab for most of the day. When it came to actually connecting the wires, Gabe retrieved his laptop from the office. The amused look she gave him didn't bother him at all. Part of being successful in life was knowing when to play to your strengths. An Olympic swimmer doesn't need to be good at tennis to go home with the gold.

Gabe answered work emails, texts, and familiarized himself with everything his people had been able to dig up on Josephine, her father, and Raymean. They took short breaks to eat, but then went right back to the lab. By that night Gabe was convinced Roy hadn't been the type to embezzle money or dumb enough to attempt to steal his own project.

Roy had been a highly decorated Army retiree. His inventions over the years focused on saving lives in and out of the military. From the lightweight, inexpensive bulletproof vest he'd sold to the US government to the individual, indestructible, water purification straw he was known for—Roy didn't appear to have profited much from his designs. He'd either been a poor businessman or it hadn't been about the money for him. For someone like Gabe, the latter was difficult to imagine. The easiest way to uncover a person's true motivation was to observe their behavior over time. Gabe hunted through Roy's past. He'd only had one credit card in his name, and it was one he'd shared with Josephine. He hadn't been in debt. No gambling problem. No known vices. Gabe's people sifted through everything Roy had purchased, driven, or rented over the last ten years. There was no hint of ego or desire to live higher than his means.

Everyone had a secret, something that could be held against them if the fight went to the trenches. As far as Gabe's team could find, Roy hadn't had one.

Unless one took into account how he'd never given Josephine credit for helping him. *If she helped him.*

Could he have died while she was trying to steal the bike?

No, that didn't make sense. She had the prototype.
According to her.
The real one might have blown up in the fire, and she's

here attempting to recreate her father's work.

He looked up from his laptop and watched her replace items on the shelves. She was meticulous, not only in location but in how they faced. It needed to be perfect. She caught him watching her and blushed beneath his attention then stood and stretched. That was all it took for his thoughts to wander below the belt.

I can't sleep with her until I know if she's still lying.

Even though we've already had sex.

In a situation such as this, would more sex with someone I've already been with count as morally wrong?

She smiled at him and his heart started to beat wildly. *If it ends up that she's some kind of serial killer, I'll deserve whatever I get because I can't stop wanting her.*

All the warning signs are here, but my dick just doesn't care.

Damn.

"I'm done for today. How about you?" she asked.

He glanced down at his laptop and the bulge in his pants beneath it. "There's nothing here I can do anything about right now, so I'm done, too." He closed his laptop and stood.

"Did you study up on magnesium-ions?" she asked with a hint of smug humor.

"Did you pick those shorts because you know your ass looks great in them?" he asked in the same tone.

Neither of them had a witty response for the other so they let both questions drift away unaddressed. They turned off the lab lights and locked the door.

They walked side by side to the main house. It was a beautiful night with a bright blanket of stars above. He was tempted to ask her if she'd like to join him on the swing again, but he didn't. The woman he'd held that night had been lying to him. *Had any of what she'd revealed been true?*

One of his men interrupted briefly to tell him they'd set up cameras on the property and wanted to know if Gabe wanted her motorcycle moved to the garage.

"Tomorrow," he said. Having it in the house was an insurance policy of sorts. He looked around and realized Josephine was gone. "Did you see where she went?" he asked abruptly.

The other man nodded at the house. "She went inside."

"Of course," Gabe said, hating the relief that filled him.

He wondered what Hunter would think of the situation he was in. *Not daring? I'm out here with a woman who may kill me in my sleep.*

And that only turns me on more.

Now who's the family daredevil?

Chapter Thirteen

THE NEXT MORNING Josephine woke before Gabe, showered quickly, and headed to her lab early. She wanted to put some time into solving the issues she faced with the power cell before she wasted the day explaining them.

She wasn't proud of how she'd bolted into the house the night before without even saying goodnight to Gabe. Her feelings for him were as tangled as a toddler's attempt at drawing a geometrical knot. Was he her lover? Captor? Judge and jury? She was about to show him research that even her father had only seen parts of. Not because she didn't trust her father, but because she'd learned not to show him the mathematical theory if it was beyond his level of understanding. He would either doubt her or himself, and she'd never wanted either.

Gabe might betray her.

Or resent her.

Her notes might mean nothing to him. She needed time to plan how to present her research to him.

I could simplify it.

Or lie.

He wouldn't know.

She paced her lab. *But I would.*

I'm already someone I don't recognize. Six months alone and thinking about nothing beyond beating Raymean has changed me.

Maybe I shouldn't trust Gabe, but who do I trust then? And if the answer is no one, then what stops me from becoming Frank? Even if I win against Raymean, if I lose myself along the way, what happens next? Do I withdraw? Close everyone out? Do I want the rest of my life to be as lonely as the last six months have been?

No.

No, I don't.

When you start with a known variable the answer to the unknown becomes obvious.

Nothing I've read about Gabe has given me any reason to doubt him. He could have turned me over to the police or thrown me off his property, but he didn't.

She turned on her computer and opened several files. She input numbers and ran a simulation, then recorded the unsatisfactory result. She read over her older notes, compared them to the results she'd had from other battery types. The discharge was simply too unpredictable under prolonged use. She didn't want something that would pass initial safety tests then fail to save a soldier in the field. Every time she'd thought she had the answer, the ratio of risk was too high.

"Not hungry this morning?" Gabe asked as he walked into the lab.

She turned in her chair so she could watch his approach. "I wanted to put some time in before showing it all to you."

He stood behind her chair and scanned the screen of her computer. "What is the major obstacle you're facing?"

She pointed to her sheet. "Magnesium batteries have been successfully developed, but not for this purpose. The lithium-ion batteries of today will one day be obsolete. The StealthOff needs to be less expensive, have a greater energy density, and not suffer the fate of ion batteries by overheating. In theory, my battery will provide twice as much electricity. The problem I'm facing is with the electrolyte itself. Increased charge causes the ions to be surrounded by oppositely charged matter or ions which reduces output. If I introduce solvent molecules or blockers, they bottleneck the output like the earth holds back magma. Discharge occurs, but right now either at dangerous or insufficient levels. If I can stabilize the discharge, I will have a working, cost-effective alternative to ion batteries. It will not only fuel the bike, but might change the transportation industry as well."

"You'd be rich overnight."

She stood. "It's not about the money."

"It's *always* about the money."

"Not for me. Not for my father. And one day, this bike will extract a fallen soldier from behind enemy lines through remote control. Do you know what that soldier won't be thinking about that day? Money. He'll be thinking about the wife he'll be able to return to and the kids who almost lost their father. Protecting the men and women who protect us is what got my father out of bed every morning. And finishing this for him is all I have left. I will not get rich from this. I don't care if I make a dime from it. When it has served its purpose and exonerated my father, I'll make sure it gets in the hands of those who will use it for our armed forces. No charge. In the name of my father."

Gabe rubbed a hand over his eyes. "I'm glad I had coffee this morning. You are wound up."

She turned away from him. "And you're an ignorant ass." *Why did I think he'd understand? He sees everything in terms of its monetary value.*

He placed a muffin beside her keyboard. "Did you have breakfast? I sound the same when I skip breakfast."

She threw the muffin at him. It bounced off his chest and fell to the floor.

"Feel better?"

She sighed. "A little, but I was aiming for your head."

He pulled up a chair next to her. "Do you know what doesn't help productivity?"

She wished she had another muffin, but she asked, "What?"

"Anger. You're angry with Raymean, your friends, me, and your father for leaving you. Even magnesium is on your shit list. How is that working for you?"

"I'm not—" She was about to say angry with her father, but she was. She hadn't realized it until Gabe said it, but she wanted to shake her father and ask him what he was doing so recklessly that it killed him. He was a scientist.

How could he leave me? He said he never would. He promised. The last thought was followed by a wave of shame. "You forgot me."

He arched an eyebrow.

"I'm angry with myself for not being able to solve this. I *should* have the answer by now. Six months. I've never made this little progress for that long."

Gabe waved a hand over the computer screen. "Josephine, you lost your dad. Yes, you've been working on this for six months, but you have also been grieving." She sucked in a deep breath and looked to the floor. *I miss my dad, and I didn't have half the relationship with him that she had with hers.* "I won't pretend the numbers make sense to me, but walk me through your process. Tell me what you have, what you don't have, and what your plan is for the next step." He took out his phone and sent a text. A moment later there was a knock on the door of the lab. One of his men had arrived with a pot of coffee and muffins. Gabe poured two coffees, placed one in front of Josephine, then placed a muffin on a napkin beside her. "Eat and talk. Don't worry about what I will or won't understand. Don't justify things to me. Just talk."

Josephine took a bite of the muffin. She'd planned to

give him an overview, but if he wanted to hear everything, she'd tell him everything. The likelihood that he'd be able to remember drastically reduced the risk of doing so. She started with how she and her father had started with an ion battery but had quickly realized it wasn't viable. Once she began listing the many combinations she'd tried, she realized how good it felt to get it out of her head. The entire project from start to present poured out of her. She thought Gabe would quickly become bored or overwhelmed, but he didn't appear to. Whenever she paused, he asked another question that revealed he was sharper than she'd given him credit for. He soaked up data and process descriptions like some people take in gossip. Hours went by. Lunch was delivered. She showed him graphs of other element ion batteries she'd reconfigured and left behind to focus on the potential of magnesium.

By evening, she felt drained and he looked tired. She hadn't discovered any answers, but it hadn't been the waste of time she'd imagined it would be. If nothing else, she'd clarified the problem to herself.

They locked the lab door and walked toward the house together. One of Gabe's men started toward them, turned around, and walked away. "Sit for a minute. I have a few final questions for you."

"You really want more?" she joked. When he didn't laugh, she took a seat on the porch swing.

He sat beside her and a memory of the last time they'd sat on the swing came back to her. She'd been as confused about what she felt for him that night as she was now. He didn't put his arm around her, and she was both relieved and disappointed.

She waited for him to ask a question, but he sat there looking at the stars as if he was in no rush to say much of anything. Her mind was racing; his appeared to have stalled. "What did you want to know?"

He looked at her. Even in the dark she saw the desire in his eyes. An answering heat rushed through her. This was the one constant in their relationship. She might not know what motivated him. He might not trust her, but they battled the same hunger. His gaze fell to her mouth, and it was impossible not to remember how good kissing him had been. She bit her bottom lip and turned to look at the stars.

He cleared his throat. "Don't answer immediately. It would be better if you gave yourself time to think your response over."

Better for me or for him? Is he going to ask me to go upstairs with him? Leave? He was using that formal tone again, which wasn't a good sign. She clasped her hands on her lap and prepared herself.

If he propositions me, I have to say no. Yes would make an already complicated situation worse.

He might be about to ask me to leave.

Please don't ask me to leave.

"I did a lot of thinking while you were talking through your research today."

She grabbed his arm and shook it. "About what? Just

ask your damn question."

HER TOUCH WAS a shock that temporarily knocked what he was about to say out of his head. There was only her and the way his body came alive beneath her caress. Okay, it wasn't so much a caress as a jostling, but it was sexy.

When it came to Josephine, everything was sexy. He hadn't thought it was possible to be turned on by scientific terms, but when they came from her sweet lips he lapped them up. *She can combine her ions with mine anytime.* He almost smiled, but she didn't look ready to appreciate the joke. It wasn't that he hadn't listened to her, but any man's mind would wander a few times during a day-long lecture of elements and their neighboring clusters.

He laid his hand over hers and stilled it. The last shred of his self-control was all that stopped him from leaning down and kissing her. "Are you okay?"

She pulled her hand back. "Sorry. I guess I'm tired."

➥ *I really am an ass. She spent the day trying to convince me that she's telling the truth. Of course she's tired and jumpy. I'd have asked the question, though, if she hadn't grabbed me. Hands to yourself, missy. I'm trying to problem solve here.* "As I was listening to you today I started thinking—are you doing everything you would have done before your father died? You said you were making better progress before. When I have difficulty with a project, the first thing I do is gather information. It seems like you've done that. Next I ask myself what is standing between me and what I want. You've done that as well. Finally, if I hit a wall, I circle back to my last success in a similar situation and look at what I'm doing differently. I understand you lost your father, and that is horrible on every level, but how else did it affect your work? Did you bounce ideas off him? Was there someone else you turned to? A friend? A colleague?"

She gave him a funny look. "You sound like you care."

"I do." Crazy as the situation was, he did.

"Does that mean you believe me?"

He pressed his lips together. He wasn't ready to go that far. "I believe you're close to solving the power issue. I believe that if you do, it could benefit many people."

She looked back up at the stars. "I haven't accessed the dark web since I've been here."

"The dark web. I read an article on it. Isn't that a hub for criminals and pedophiles?"

"Yes and no. It simply means it's not searchable and the users are usually untraceable. There are deeper levels than your average criminal would know how to access. What you're referring to is the layer just off the grid. Anyone who wants to be anonymous and has basic computer skills can go there. I'm talking about the deeper web where people use encryptions so secure most governments couldn't crack them. I normally would have taken this problem there and incorporated some of their ideas into my testing."

He didn't understand. "So, let me get this straight, you'd post your research on the web and work off anonymous tips?" Not a sound process in his opinion.

She shook her head. "I have a closed network of contacts who exchange ideas with me. I know who they are."

Something in her voice prompted him to ask, "Do they know who *you* are?"

"No. I've been very careful. They think I'm actually three people."

Here we go down the rabbit hole. "How do you know they're any more honest than you are?"

"I personally invited each of them to join the network based on years of communication and collaboration."

"As yourself or an alias?"

"As whoever I thought they would talk to."

Shit. "Is this where I find out Josephine isn't your real name?"

She let out a shaky breath. "I don't expect you to believe me, but I'm being completely honest with you—more honest than I've been with anyone. When I was in my teens, my father was shot and injured because the Army couldn't afford a bulletproof vest for him. I knew I had to do something. He had an idea for a cheaper material, but his wasn't fail-safe. I understood the problem, but I didn't have the knowledge base to help him so I wrote to some of the top people in the field. I knew they wouldn't talk to a high school student so I lied about who I was. In the beginning I was a professor at a university in Europe. Then I was a top-secret government think-tank participant. It didn't matter who I said I was, the ideas we exchanged were real. I took what I learned back to my father and that was his ticket out of the military. I went back and shared what I'd learned with the others. They started asking me questions, and it evolved over the years. I've known them for over a decade, and I have helped each of them as much as they've helped me. You could ask any of them and they'd tell you that."

"I could ask anonymous people online to vouch for you even though none of them know your real name?" He heard the skepticism in his own voice.

She deflated beside him. "You asked me what I've done differently this time, and I told you the truth. I usually run ideas by them but I haven't, not since I've been here."

He hated to see her sad almost as much as he hated the idea that she could still be lying to him. He took her hand in his and laced his fingers through hers. He didn't know much about the dark web, but he had built a solid company by building and maintaining a variety of networks. No, not a geek squad like she was describing, but that didn't change the fundamentals of where her process had failed. "You closed yourself off from your network. That's why you're not moving forward. You're attempting to do in isolation what you used to do in collaboration."

She was quiet a long time. "I was afraid to bring it to them. My father's death was well publicized. Everyone knows what he was working on. If I take this to the network, they could figure out who I am."

"Why would that be such a bad thing? You just said these people are indebted to you. You've been handling this alone when you may, in fact, have allies."

She looked down at their linked hands. "I have trust issues."

"No kidding?" *So do I, but this shit has to be real. Who could make this up?* "You need to tell them who you are."

"It's not that easy," she said.

"Unless it is. You said you know these people. Do they have a reputation for stealing the ideas of others? How cut-throat are they?"

"They're philosophers, physicists, doctors, engineers. They don't need to steal ideas; their names will already go down as some of the greatest minds of our time."

"So the only thing holding you back is fear."

She elbowed him. "You're such an ass."

He smiled. "A pattern is emerging. You swear at me when I'm right."

"Oh, I'll swear at you."

His hand tightened on hers. He wagged his eyebrows at her. "Do it, I'd love it."

She laughed, and he let go of her hand to swing his arm over her shoulder. She tensed, then relaxed against his side. "What if Raymean finds out I'm still pursuing this? What if they find me? You?"

He was willing to shoulder that and anything else as long as she stayed right there in his arms. He kissed her forehead and said, "You're safe, Josephine."

She snuggled closer to him. "I want to believe that."

He didn't move, opting instead to simply hold her. Wanting something to be true didn't make it so. Not for her and not for him. He wasn't a gambling man. He didn't put himself in situations where the outcome was this unpredictable.

He looked up at the sky and said, "I used to know the names of all the constellations. Amazing what you can forget when remembering isn't relevant." It was a white lie, but he guessed she wouldn't be able to resist showing him that she knew them. It was a side of her he doubted he'd ever tire of. She was truly brilliant but with a humility that was endearing.

She tentatively started to point them out to him. He hugged her closer, letting himself enjoy the feel of her in his arms and the soothing tone of her voice.

Chapter Fourteen

THE NEXT MORNING, with Gabe sitting next to her, answering his own emails, Josephine wrote a long letter of explanation and posted it on the encrypted message board her network used. She apologized for never being forthright with her real name and explained why. She briefly described the wall she had hit with her prototype power cell and requested fresh eyes.

A moment later a message came in from one of the first scientists she'd contacted, a physicist from Yale. He said her identity was irrelevant in the face of her contributions to the community. He promised to think about the problem and send suggestions. He said the world had lost a great creative mind when her father had died, but it was a relief to know she wasn't Roy. When news of his death had spread, and all contact with her had ended, the network had assumed she was Roy. The email ended by saying, "None of us believed your father was a fraud."

Another email came in with a much more eloquently worded message that said essentially the same thing.

Josephine burst into grateful tears. When Gabe

looked over in concern, she waved dismissively. "It's good. It's so good."

She read the emails to him and loved that he seemed proud of her. *Does it matter if something is wrong when it's this right?* She leaned over, whispered, "Thank you," and kissed him.

He pulled back in shock.

What am I thinking? He doesn't trust me with the keys to anything because he thinks I could be a criminal. Do I actually believe he's still interested in me?

"I have never felt lower than I did after we were together the first time. Are you sure?" he asked.

"I am." His concern fanned her confidence. "I'm me now. This time we wouldn't have the lies. This time would be real."

"I want you so much I can barely think, but I don't want to hurt you."

"Sometimes a little hurt feels good." She winked and his expression changed. Gone was the tentative man. Gabe pulled her to him and kissed her hungrily. They began tearing at each other's clothing. She couldn't get enough of him or give enough of herself to him. His mouth was everywhere. Her hands sought to free him. This was no gentle lovemaking. This was an explosion of pent-up mutual lust.

She caressed the eager hardness of him. He undid the front of her shorts and delved into her wet sex. His fingers were not enough. She needed more of him.

Their feverish kisses turned to an exchange of moans

when he lifted and turned her so her back was propped against the wall, and he thrust upward into her. She still had her shirt and bra on. He had his trousers around his ankles. Nothing mattered beyond the connection they shared and how completely he filled her.

He kissed his way down her neck, tore open her shirt, and suckled her through the thin material of her bra. She clung to him, arching to give him more access to anything he wanted. That was the power of their passion. Everything fell away in the face of it. She wasn't worried that he didn't believe her. All she could think about was how much she didn't want him to stop. When his mouth moved upward and claimed hers again, she buried her hands in his hair and kissed him desperately.

Faster and faster. Harder and deeper. He took her with the hot, unrestrained passion she'd always dreamed of. She came and he followed a few strokes later. They stood there, catching their breath against each other.

He slowly lowered her to the floor. He looked down in a daze at his pants around his ankles and pulled them up before meeting her eyes. What she saw warmed her heart. He looked uncertain, which made sense considering how she'd acted after the first time they'd had sex.

She grabbed his tie and pulled his mouth down to within an inch of hers. "That was amazing."

His face transformed with a huge smile. "You have quite a way of showing your gratitude."

"Only with you," she said huskily.

He grabbed her naked ass and hauled her against

him. "Good." His hand slid between them and into her wet center. "I want to watch you come this time."

She could barely breathe when his finger began to circle her clit. Heat began to build within her again. He took a step back and sat down on a chair, pulling her across his lap, facing him. It spread her wider for him and she steadied herself with a hand on his shoulder.

She threw her shirt to the floor, unclasped her bra, and tossed it aside as well. Fully naked on a man who was dressed should have been embarrassing but she felt sexy and powerful. His mouth loved one bare breast then the other. Wherever his mouth trailed, pleasure followed. All the while his hand brought her closer and closer to losing control.

When she threw her head back and clenched on his fingers he raised his head. "Come for me, Josie."

This time the name didn't bother her. It wasn't a lie any more, it was a nickname. She'd never had one and was discovering she liked it. He knew her better than any man ever had. He could call her anything he wanted.

She cried out in release and the door of the lab flew open. One of Gabe's men said, "Sorry, boss, I thought—" He didn't say more, choosing instead to make a hasty retreat and slam the door behind him.

Josephine didn't know whether to laugh or cry. Gabe helped her off him and stood. He dropped his pants to the floor, stepping out of them this time. His shaft stood proudly erect and ready for round two.

Security man? What security man?

LATER THAT NIGHT Gabe held Josephine in his arms while she slept. She'd been shy at first about joining him in his room, but he wore her resistance down in the best possible manner. He was enjoying his reward, the feel of her naked body cuddled against his.

He could only imagine what the women he'd dated over the years would think of him when it came to Josephine. He'd escorted enough of them to the door while explaining that, although he enjoyed their company, he needed his space as well. It was completely different with Josephine. Every time she left the room he wasn't sure she was coming back. Every time she came back, he hated the idea of her leaving again. She was every bit the addiction he'd called her.

A brilliant, sexy, troubled addiction. He'd never been one to hold on to anything or anyone, which was obvious in his initial reaction to sell the ranch, but he felt different around her. She was a high that energized him, made him feel that anything was possible. His staff joked that ranch life must be good for him because he'd reeled in the key foreign clients and more. He normally worked much slower, methodically, making very few moves he hadn't thoroughly investigated. He'd taken a few risks this time, and they had paid off.

Could a real estate man have a muse? She felt like one. He'd thought working from a satellite office would hinder his ability to oversee his team, but instead it freed him to focus on the bigger picture and delegate the mundane aspects of relocating to Silicon Valley. He'd never considered himself a micro-manager, but his teams were thriving under his less controlling direction.

As his company had grown, his role had changed. He brokered multi-million-dollar estates and corporate land deals. In the beginning he'd been involved in all aspects of moving the properties, but he'd moved to more of a spearhead role. He cleared the way for his people to work in a new market. He dealt with politicians who might try to block a sale or purchase. Most recently that role had gone international, involving governments and growing his network internationally.

I can do all of that from here for a month.

And then what?

He slid out of bed, careful not to wake her, and threw on a pair of sweats. He headed to his father's office. The hour of night was irrelevant; Gabe had things he needed to set into motion, and they would be easier to organize while Josephine slept.

He called Andre Woods, the head of his security team, who was smart enough to pick up.

Gabe had a great respect for Andre's ability to get things done and to do so without the need of time-consuming social niceties. "What did you find out about Frank Muller?"

Andre's voice went from groggy to businesslike as he spoke. "Small-time inventor of household conveniences. Lives mostly off the grid. Supplements the small income he makes from the sales of early inventions by working as a caretaker or house-sitter. He was hired as a caretaker of the ranch five years ago by the property management company your father used. That business went under, but Frank stayed on."

"His connection to Roy Ashby?"

"Nothing beyond that they grew up in the same town."

"Anything new about Raymean and Roy Ashby?"

"No one's talking. First responders to the scene are tight-lipped. There is nothing to disprove Raymean's version of what happened, but also nothing that confirms it. No photos. No video. It's all too neat. Too tight. Sounds scripted that they're all saying the same thing. Want me to dig deeper?"

Gabe thought about the woman sleeping in his bed upstairs. Mostly believing her wasn't good enough. "There was or is a video of what happened in Ashby's lab the night he died. What would you need to get me either the video or proof of what was on it?"

Andre answered without hesitation. "Money. The people I talked to didn't look scared, they looked bought. Throw sufficient cash at them and someone will talk. But know that there might be consequences."

"I'll handle the consequences. What kind of money are we talking about?"

"I won't know for sure until I make them an offer and see their reaction. My guess is you're looking at five, maybe six figures. How high do you want me to go?"

"For a first-hand account that's reasonable, stay in five figures. For the video, go to seven figures if you need to. I want to know what happened that night, but I want to see it with my own eyes or it's worth next to nothing to me."

"Understood."

"And, Andre, I need more men down here. Well-paid and well-armed."

"You'll have them by tomorrow morning. Something happen? My last report said all was quiet."

"It has been so far, but I may have just given her location up. I don't know. I'm still trying to figure out exactly how dark that dark web is."

Andre cleared his throat. "I have to throw this out there. Are you sure she's worth it? This isn't a dirty politician you're taking on. Raymean not only has money, it has an army of lawyers. You're waking a giant."

"Do you think Raymean had Roy Ashby killed?"

"They're hiding something."

"Find out what and make sure it doesn't get us all killed."

"I need a raise," Andre joked.

"Bring me that video and you'll have it."

After hanging up with Andre, Gabe went back upstairs and slid into bed beside Josephine. She moaned, turned over, and threw an arm around his waist. He ran his hand lightly through her hair.

Andre said I might be waking a giant, but the giant took something that didn't belong to him. When he thought back to Josephine's impassioned plea, he was moved. Again. *"Protecting the men and women who protect us is what got my father out of bed every morning. And finishing this for him is all I have left."*

Gabe thought about his brothers who had served in the military. He wanted to believe that there were good people out there who supported the armed forces—supported what his brothers had done out of a sense of duty.

This isn't about money. Not for her. Not for me.

I believe her.

You're safe now, Josie.

And we'll find out what happened to your father.

Chapter Fifteen

MIDDAY THE NEXT day, Josephine paused while inputting data into her computer. She wasn't used to smiling as she worked, but she knew she was. Gabe had made a place for himself in the corner of her lab. Everything felt possible with him by her side. Hope had replaced desperation. Passion had eviscerated loneliness.

He looked up from working online and returned her smile. From the way his gaze ran over her, she wondered if he was remembering the slow lovemaking they'd started their day with or the rough and wild sex that had followed in the shower. She couldn't have said which she'd enjoyed more because every time with Gabe was different and wonderful in its own way.

"What are you thinking?" he asked in that deep, gravelly voice of his.

"Naughty, naughty thoughts," she joked and winked.

His smile widened. "Great minds think alike." He nodded at her computer. "Are you making any progress?"

"Not yet, but I'm turning my testing to the relation-ship between electrolytes and the magnesium ions when they shed their coordination spheres. Primarily the first sphere since that has the greater influence on the reactivity and chemical properties."

He cocked his head to one side. "Coordination spheres?"

"The metal atom plus the ligands that are bonded to it," she added and waited. "The molecules that attach themselves to the metal."

"Ligands?"

"A molecule that binds to another molecule."

"Molecule?" he asked with a straight face, and she realized he was playing with her. If she'd had something to throw at him, she would have.

Instead she decided to give him some of his own medicine. "Let me see if I can explain this better." She made her voice low and sexy. "Hi, I'm a metal atom, and I want to bond with an ion. I want it so, so bad. I crave his electron pairs. I want him around me. Not just any ligand. It has to be the right one or my performance won't be stable. So I'm stripping and inserting different solvents because too hot/too fast is disappointing. I want this coupling to go all night when I need it to."

Gabe loosened his tie. "You can talk science to me any day. That's how all science classes should be taught. I was expecting the atom to add: Although if you were my teacher, I'd want you naked."

She laughed both because of his joke and because being with him made her feel young and sexy. It was not only exciting, but also fun.

She didn't allow herself to fixate on the situation that

had brought them together. He wasn't stopping her from moving forward with her goal, but in fact, by encouraging her to reach out to her network, he'd given her project new life. Her online contacts hadn't solved her problem, but they'd asked questions that would broaden her testing.

"How is your work going?" she asked.

He glanced down at his laptop and then back at her. "A failed government coup in a country where a client of mine was hoping to relocate one of his factories put the deal on hold." He rubbed his chin. "I would try to make that sound sexy, but what if I just flex?" He lifted an arm and reached for a water bottle while flexing the muscles in his arm. "Does that do it for you?"

She laughed again. Gabe was as beautifully complicated as the atom structure solution of any decagonal quasicrystal. Just when she thought she understood him, she saw another side to him. He was physically stunning, which should have given him a huge ego, but hadn't. He was intelligent and successful but had a limited working understanding of the nature of what she was trying to do. Some men might have been intimidated when involved in something outside their area of expertise, but Gabe took their differences in stride—even found humor in them. That required real confidence and, man—that was sexy as all hell.

She had a hard time finding a single fault in him, outside of the fact that he hadn't said he believed her. It felt too good to be true, but she didn't question it because she didn't want to. She already knew what it was like to be afraid, completely alone, and to have had her heart broken by those she thought she could trust.

Even if I discover that Gabe isn't the man I think he is, I need this. I need to remember what it was like to believe in someone—anyone.

"You'll notice a few more men around here today," he said.

She didn't want to ask, but she needed to. "Why? Did you hear something?"

He stood, walked over to where she was sitting, and held out a hand to her. She took it and rose to her feet before him. "I told you I'd keep you safe. That's what I'm doing. You don't have to look over your shoulder anymore. Work on your battery. Prove what your father said could be done is actually possible. Let me worry about the rest."

She searched his face. She'd never had anyone look after her. Even with her father, Josephine had always been the caretaker. She'd never had anyone she could lean on. She didn't have the words to express how much she wanted what he was offering, so she wrapped her arms around his neck and pulled his mouth down to hers.

She put all of her feelings into that kiss: her hope, her fear, her gratitude. She'd never been in love, but she felt herself falling into that kiss, into him. His kiss was bold and consuming. It left no room for anything but complete submission and ownership, but it created a need in her that only he could fulfill.

As her clothing fell to the floor, his mouth worshipped each new area revealed. She was quivering with desire and blindly undressing him when she heard him softly tell her to slow down. She didn't. She couldn't. She was afraid if either of them stopped long enough to think about what they were doing together it would end.

She sank to her knees and took him deeply into her mouth. He moaned and dug his hands into her hair. "Don't listen to me, Josie, go as fast or slow as you want. Just don't stop."

OVER THE NEXT two weeks, Gabe and Josephine fell into a deeply satisfying pattern. During the day they worked side by side in her lab, spicing the day up with work breaks that left both of them sweaty, sated, and smiling. Every evening they enjoyed another aspect of the ranch. Slowly, in ways that disturbed neither their work nor their pleasure, Gabe was having the ranch updated. The pool was cleaned and filled. Fresh coats of paint brought a shine to areas that had begun to show signs of neglect. On the outside the ranch was beginning to look the way Gabe felt on the inside—new, fresh. Losing his father and finding Josephine had brought life to a part of Gabe he hadn't known he'd starved.

Two weeks and he wanted to be with her every bit as much as the day he'd met her. The sex was amazing, but their connection was deeper. He'd dated intelligent women, but Josephine was a genius. A humble one.

When she'd said the greatest minds of their time turned to her for advice, he'd thought she was enhancing the truth to impress him. Time beside her at the lab had taught him that if anything she undersold herself and her network. No wonder her father had kept her out of the limelight. Someone like her would be gobbled up by a government agency, especially if they knew how much influence she had in everything from biochemistry to satellite technology. They'd want to control her.

Our kids will be brilliant.

One evening, during a walk, he asked her what she wanted after she cleared her father's name. "Would you start your own company? Go after a military contract? The world knew your father. They could know you now."

She skipped a stone across the creek and took a moment before answering. "I had a very brief taste of what people would call normal when my dad and I lived in Connecticut. I had friends and a home for the first time. I don't want to be known, I want to be normal. Is that crazy? Christmas has always been about just my dad and me. This will be my first one without him." She blinked back tears. "I hope I don't spend it alone."

He took her hand and raised it to his lips. For a long time, the holiday had meant next to nothing to him, but he wanted to give her what she'd never had. "We'll spend it together."

She smiled sadly. "You don't have to promise me anything. I've been living day to day for so long I'm used to it. I wouldn't even be thinking about the holidays if you hadn't asked what I want."

He turned and kissed her lightly on the lips then. "You need to believe in me."

Another small smile. "I do? Why?"

"Because I believe in you."

She burst into tears and threw herself into his arms. He'd grown up in a household of men so he wasn't entirely sure but he thought that was a good sign.

They made love near the spot where he'd once broken his arm, proving conclusively that the view from the ground had more potential than the treetop ever would. On the way back to the main house, Gabe's phone rang. When he saw the caller, he froze. Andre. He'd said he'd call as soon as he knew something. Gabe's expression must have revealed something because Josephine's hand tensed in his.

"Who is it?" she asked in a concerned tone.

He dropped her hand and waved for her to go inside. "Work. I'll join you in a few minutes."

She looked like she wanted to ask him more, but she didn't. "Is everything fine with the office move? I know some people who could help with the computer system if you're still having issues with it."

The call went through to his messages unanswered. He wasn't about to take that call in front of her. "No, we resolved the glitch. Go inside. I'll be right in."

"Okay," she said reluctantly. Her instincts were too damn good.

As soon as the door closed behind Josephine, Gabe returned Andre's call. "Did you find anything?"

"Yes, but it's not what I expected."

Chapter Sixteen

JOSEPHINE PACED THE living room floor while waiting
for Gabe to join her. She liked to think she was a
confident, modern woman who could face anything. Her
stomach had twisted into a ball of knots as soon as Gabe
had turned his phone away so she couldn't see the caller
ID.

Two weeks of working side by side had given Josephine a false sense of security. She'd thought Gabe
hadn't hidden anything from her. He'd talked to his
team, his clients, even some adversaries. She'd heard him
negotiate, placate, and threaten. Until that moment she'd
thought they didn't have secrets from each other.

But we do.

If Josephine had been the paranoid type, she would
have bugged his phone. She'd had enough access to his
technology and knew people who could help her hack
into them without him ever knowing. She hadn't done
any of that, though, because she trusted him.

Who would he not want me to know he's talking to?

Someone at Raymean?

Another woman?

Both possibilities played to fears she'd tried to convince herself she didn't have. She'd stabilized her power cell, at least in computer simulations. It was time to test it out on the bike itself. Although she'd told Gabe she was close to the solution, she hadn't told him exactly how close. She wanted to surprise him by whizzing by him on the StealthOff. When she fantasized about that moment, she'd imagined two versions—one where she rode by looking amazing in an all-black, skintight suit and the other where she was naked. Both scenarios culminated in an erotic celebration of her discovery.

Does he know how close I am? Is he reporting to someone who wants the power cell?

Or worse.

Well, not sure if it's worse, but it would kill me in another way.

Two weeks into a four-week stay on the ranch, is he getting sick of me? Is he talking to whoever he'll return to when he goes home?

Why would he say all the wonderful things he does if he doesn't mean them?

Isn't that what all women ask themselves when they discover the man they're falling in love with isn't falling in love with them? What the heck am I doing?

Falling in love?

She sat on a chair. She let her head hang between her legs and took several deep breaths. *Oh, my God. I'm falling in love.*

Should I tell him?

Would that change his mind if he's just about to turn me and my research over to someone in exchange for money?

Josephine hadn't grown up with girlfriends she confided in. She grasped wildly at dark questions. *Does he have someone else? Would hearing that I love him keep him out of the arms of another woman?*

She felt like she was going to throw up, so she rushed to the downstairs bathroom and bent over the toilet. When nothing came up, she washed her face off with a wet cloth and looked herself in the eye in the mirror above the sink. *Don't do this. Don't assume something is bad simply because he doesn't want to share it.*

He hasn't done a single suspicious thing.

Except attach himself to me instantly and not leave. He says it's because he enjoys being with me that much, but what if it's because he wants to watch me?

He has money of his own. He wouldn't be on Raymean's payroll. Would he?

What if not all of his money is from his company? He has all kinds of connections. If he told anyone about what I'm working on they would have told him how much it was worth.

Too good to be true . . .

Which is more likely? That I met a man who instantly fell for me and will do anything for me?

Or that my lonely state left me vulnerable to being manipulated by someone who wants to profit from my work?

My father would have said I was being paranoid.

You should have listened to me, Dad.

Josephine moved to a corner of the room where she could watch Gabe. He was off the phone and talking to one of his men on the porch. She crawled over to the window next to where they were and listened.

"While I'm gone you need to make sure she doesn't leave the ranch."

"Understood."

Gabe sighed. "Is there any way we could cut off communication to the ranch and make it look like a power outage? It'll need to happen in town so she's not suspicious. Her cell phone relies on the Internet working. Once it goes down, she's going to get antsy. She's smart; you'll have to be smarter. Make sure none of the vehicles work, but don't give her a hint that anything is out of the ordinary."

"Copy that. To clarify, we shoot to kill."

"If necessary, yes."

Josephine gasped and covered her mouth with her hand. *Shoot to kill? Shoot. To. Kill?* Of all the things she'd worried about, she'd never thought Gabe would be planning to kill her. She couldn't imagine the man she'd given herself to so intimately would ever hurt her.

But betray me? I guess I always knew he would.

Everyone eventually does.

She stood and caught her breath. *This is what happens when you sleep with a man you hardly know.*

She laughed without humor.

Actually, this doesn't happen. This is worse than what happens. I wish I were only finding out that he's married or jobless.

She ran his plan over in her head and began to plot one of her own. By the time Gabe entered the house a cold calm had settled over her.

"Sorry it took so long," he said. "It ended up more complicated than I thought."

She forced a smile. "That's okay. I'm fighting a raging headache. That latest test was a complete flop."

He frowned. "Was it? You were so hopeful."

"Yes, that's how it goes. One leap forward, one slide back. Looks like I'm not as close as I thought."

He looped his hands around her waist and kissed her forehead. "I'm sorry to hear that. You'll figure it out."

"Yes, I will," she said with more emotion than she meant to.

"I need to leave for a couple of days. You'll be fine, though. Julio and Dez will be here with you."

"What about the occupancy clause?"

"I'm allowed to leave for a few days here and there. It'll be fine."

"Where are you going?" She tried to sound casual.

"There's something I need to handle back at the office that can't be done over the phone." He wasn't an accomplished liar like she was. He looked guilty, but she pretended not to notice.

She wanted to push him for more, but that would increase the risk of him knowing that she'd heard his plan. Instead, she kept smiling and purred, "I'll miss you."

His expression relaxed. "I'll miss you, too. I was going to leave in the morning."

She made a show of rubbing her temples. "Go tonight if it's urgent. I'll be fine. Well, once I get rid of this headache."

He laid a hand across her temple. "You don't feel feverish, but I'll bring you some Tylenol. You've been working nonstop for two weeks. You're probably exhausted. I can leave tomorrow. I'll stay and make sure you're okay."

She shook her head. "No, no. It's just a simple headache. I'll sleep in, relax tomorrow, and be better by the time you return."

"If you're sure."

This is where I prove that I lie better than you do. "I'm sure, but knowing I have you to take care of me makes me feel a little better already."

GABE LEFT HIS car at the ranch and flew out on a private plane to Connecticut. He hated the idea of leaving Josephine, but he didn't want to risk her getting hurt if things went south. Andre met him at the airport and drove him to the hotel room he'd rented for the next two days.

The sun was high in the sky by the time Andre plugged a flash drive into Gabe's laptop. "I'll warn you, it's pretty graphic."

Gabe took the computer and settled down onto the couch with it. For the first few minutes the only person on the video was Ashby. He typed on his computer, poured a glass of water from the water cooler, and returned to work at his computer. Gabe glanced across at Andre.

"I didn't edit any of it out. I wanted to make sure it was a clean copy."

Gabe looked back down at the video. Ashby took a phone call. "I'm still at the lab. Of course I'll come. I'll leave now."

The lights were turned off and the screen went black. A few minutes later the lights came back on and a man in his twenties, wearing a baseball cap that concealed his face from the camera, came in. He hunted around on the desk until he found a key. He put a flash drive in Ashby's computer before walking out of view again. When he returned he was pushing a bike that looked identical to the one Josephine was working on. He looked up quickly and drew a gun.

Ashby walked back into the view of the security camera. "Get off that bike."

"You shouldn't have come back, old man. I wanted to do this without hurting anyone."

Ashby walked forward with his hands raised. "You still can. This is a mistake. Put the damn gun away and get off the bike. My daughter is older than you. You've got your whole life ahead of you. Don't throw it away on something like this."

The young man waved his gun wildly at Ashby. "I can't let you live. Why did you have to come back?" He started the bike.

Ashby took another step forward. "Son, that bike is only a prototype. It's not even the most advanced one. Killing me won't get you what you want. Get off the bike. If you need money or something I could help you."

"I don't need your help. I need you to shut up." He waved the gun again and Ashby stepped closer.

"Son, if you're thinking of escaping on that bike the engine will overheat in less than ten miles and that battery will go up like a mini napalm. You won't make it anywhere."

The man shot at something in what had probably been an attempt to scare him, but Ashby took the opening to grab the gun, locked it, and tossed it to the far corner of the room. "Get off the bike. I may be old, but you're asking for a good old-fashioned ass kicking."

The young man revved the bike's engine, but he looked scared. "I didn't want to kill you, but I'm leaving with this bike. Let me go and you won't get hurt."

He went to drive by Ashby, but the old man had more military than civilian in him. He lunged, grabbed the arm of the man, and sent both crashing to the floor. The young man tried to punch Ashby, but Ashby blocked it. Ashby gave him a punch to the face that sent the young man to his knees then hauled him to his feet. "Sometimes a man has to find his knees before he can change his life." He punched him again and the man sank to the floor. "Consider this your rock bottom and pull your life together. I don't know what brought you here, son, but everyone has a choice. Make your next one a good one."

Ashby went to the bike and turned it off. Gabe cringed when the young man scrambled to his feet and grabbed the gun again. He fumbled to unlock it and pointed it at Ashby. "This time I'll do it. I will."

He shot and the bike exploded.

The two men must have died instantly because there was no sound on the video, only smoke and flames, followed by an alarm going off and the sprinkler system going on.

Several moments later, security guards were using fire extinguishers on the fire and not making much headway. Someone said the fire department was on its way. A bald man in a suit began barking questions. "No. That's not how this will go down. Get that body and the gun out of here."

The security men shook their heads and that enraged the bald man. He threatened everything from their jobs to their families. An evil look twisted his expression, and he offered a bribe of a hundred thousand each, making it worth their while to hide the truth. By the time the firefighters arrived, the fire was out and the bald man was telling them a tale of how Ashby had been caught in the act of trying to steal the prototype.

"Who is that?" Gabe asked Andre, who was standing beside the couch.

"Felix Zainer, head of Product Development at Raymean. He's been with the company since its early days and was pissed when the founder retired and handed the reins over to his son and not him. He'd brought Ashby on and invested loads of money into his program, although if you follow the money trail very little of it actually got to Ashby. My guess is Zainer was taking what he considered his due."

"Which is why he wanted it to look like Ashby was a fraud, so when the books were looked over he could claim Ashby stole it."

"That's what I'm thinking."

"Do you think the cover-up goes higher than him?"

Andre shook his head. "This weasel was planning to cut and run before the bike blew up. He was working alone. I doubt the new CEO, Don Theroux, knows. If he does, I haven't seen him act to help or stop him. He looked sincerely shocked by how Ashby had died. He was as shocked as Zainer that his father gave him the company. I hear he is barely in control of his secretary. I don't think he could pull anything like this off."

"Who was the younger guy with the gun?"

"He was on Zainer's payroll. Looks like the original plan was to frame Ashby and take off while the heat was on him."

"I need a shower, a fresh suit, and a car."

"What are you going to do?"

"I'm going to pay Theroux a visit. If he's smart he'll let Zainer, and everyone who helped him, hang."

Andre whistled. "You missed your calling when you chose real estate. You have a knack for espionage."

Gabe flexed his shoulders. "Real estate is cutthroat. Did you forget that mobster in Detroit who tried to block us from selling that property in the south end?"

"Vinnie Donlonnie? His family was in the mob a hundred years ago. That guy was barely eighteen and a two-bit, drug-dealing punk who didn't want to lose his best heroin-selling corner. I had the police visit his grandmother and offered them enough money to relocate out of the city. She took him to live with her sister."

With a shrug, Gabe removed his tie. "Don't kill my mojo before I take on Theroux."

Andre smiled, then did his best to look serious. "If you tell Theroux you've toppled mob kings, he'll probably shit himself."

"Fresh suit and a car," Gabe said. "Now."

Andre had worked for him long enough to hold off laughing until Gabe was mostly out of earshot.

Chapter Seventeen

*F*OUR ARMED SECURITY *men with orders to shoot to kill. One working vehicle that hasn't been tested. No access to my gun. Soon no access to my phone or Internet.*

Josephine didn't attempt to sleep that night. She sat in her room and methodically went through each of her options. She could reach out to her online network for help, but they weren't the heroic type. One was in his eighties. She could call the police, but what would she say?

Hi. I'm being held here against my will. Why? Oh, I can't tell you why. You'd arrest me if you knew what I'm working on. Did I call you? Never mind.

All I have is the element of surprise.

She'd wasted over an hour asking herself who Gabe was going to meet and why he would want her kept on the ranch. Each possible scenario was darker than the last until she'd been paralyzed with fear.

It was then that she'd remembered what her father had always said about fear being the enemy's greatest weapon. *I won't give them that power, Dad. I'll fight.*

Each security man was wired with a radio. *I'll have to*

disable them. Or interfere with their transmissions. How do I do that without making them suspicious?

A plan began to form in her head. *I wait until they knock out the electricity. People don't know how things work. If it happens simultaneously, they'll think they're responsible. All I have to do is find a receiver strong enough for their transmitters to lock on to. Radio silence is hardly ever noticed. My receiver will need to be battery operated so it runs when the power goes down. Luckily I have still have Internet access.*

What do I know about taking down four men? What had Gabe said, "What I can google tonight."

After doing a quick search and deciding she had all the necessary components, she looked up the best way to restrain someone. Zip ties or duct tape. Perfect. She had both in her lab. While she was searching she came across easy snare traps and was glad end-of-the-world preppers were generous with their advice. The lab made the most amount of sense as far as where to disable the men. They wouldn't suspect anything she did in there and then all she had to do was lure them in.

When she left tomorrow, there wouldn't be time to pack up her lab. Her research and the bike would have to be enough.

In the early morning hours, Josephine stripped her hair of color then dyed it blonde. It wasn't her natural, richer honey color, but it would have to do. She packed what she could into a duffel bag and chose practical clothing for her escape: running shoes, shorts, and a tight-fitting tank top. The less anyone had to grab onto the better.

She was on her way to the kitchen because keeping her routine the same would bring less attention to her. The men usually took shifts: Montee and Kyle slept during the day and swapped off in the evening with Julio and Dez. That morning, however, they all were gathered in the hallway of the house having a conversation that ended abruptly when she appeared. She smiled brightly at them. "Good morning."

"Good morning," they answered in unison.

"I hit a snag in my work yesterday, so I'll probably be in the lab all day today trying to make up the time I lost. I hate to ask, but could one of you bring me lunch around noon? I'll forget to eat if you don't, and that always makes me lightheaded." Sweet and helpless was the vibe she was trying for and it seemed to work. Dez said his girlfriend was the same way when she didn't eat and promised to bring her some protein and a salad.

"Thank you," Josephine said and shook herself inwardly when she started to relax. *Dez isn't being kind; he's probably going to use that time to check in on me. They have orders to shoot me if I try to leave. Just because they seem nice doesn't mean they are. Being gullible will get you killed.*

Julio stepped forward. "One thing you should know."

Josephine froze. "Yes?"

"When I was in town yesterday I heard the area is

having sweeping power blackouts. They don't last long, but you may want to backup whatever you're working on. And have a flashlight ready in the lab so you're not scared if the lights go out."

"I haven't heard a thing about that, but thanks for the heads-up. I'll definitely do that." She blinked back tears. Gabe was exactly who she'd feared he was.

Julio nodded and ducked his head. "You know where we are if you need us."

"Are all four of you up for the day?"

Montee shot the other men a look Josephine interpreted as, "Go along with this." He said, "Once a month some of us work double shifts so we have time to talk about how to work better together. Hey, nice hair. Blonde looks good on you."

She shrugged. "Thanks. I like to mix things up."

Kyle nodded in an exaggerated manner. "Great. We'll go back to work. We're all here if anything unusual happens. Not that it will. We don't expect anything to happen. It's a normal day."

Dez rolled his eyes skyward. "Do you need anything, Josephine, or are you all set?"

She rounded her eyes innocently. "I can't imagine what I'd need. Thank you in advance for the salad. I'll see the rest of you tonight when I finish for the day."

They each wished her a good or productive day and walked away. Josephine made herself a cup of coffee but her hands were shaking too much to hold it so she left it on the counter and headed to her lab.

Zip ties. Duct tape. Strong, thin rope for the snare. I could make a Taser. Download and erase my research from what I'm leaving behind. Build the radio receiver. Hang the snare. Put gas in the bike. I don't need to use the power cell. If all goes well, I won't need to be quiet when I run. The regular motor will get me where I need to go just fine. Money. IDs. Change of clothes. Clean underwear.

I can do this.

The power cell is good enough to take to Raymean, so maybe all of this is for the best. I'd be scared if I had anything left to lose.

I will clear your name, Dad, or die trying.

LATER THAT DAY, seated across from Theroux in the man's enormous office at Raymean, Gabe felt a moment of pity for him. He was clearly overwhelmed by the responsibility of taking over his father's company and looked a good ten years older than he should have. Nervous sweat beaded on his forehead as he watched the video. "That's how Ashby died?"

"Do you expect me to believe you didn't know?"

"I didn't. I swear I didn't." He gulped visibly. "Why would Felix do it? Why cover up what happened? It was a robbery. Not our fault."

"Ten million dollars was earmarked for the production of StealthOff. Eight hundred thousand made it into the hands of Ashby. Look over your books and you'll find nine million dollars unaccounted for. Zainer was preparing to run with the money before this went down.

He used the explosion and Ashby's death to cover his crime."

Theroux used his sleeve to wipe more sweat from his brow. "Oh, God. This will send our stocks plummeting."

"You have the video. You must have connections with the local police. Or better yet, the FBI. You need to have Zainer picked up unaware. If you do this right, you could be a hero."

Theroux loosened his tie as if it were choking him. He called his secretary and asked if she would have Zainer come see him at his earliest convenience. Gabe took the phone from Theroux and said, "Have him come now."

"I'm sorry, but Mr. Zainer hasn't shown up at the office for the last two days. No one knows where he went. He's not answering his phone."

A cold feeling swept through Gabe. "Where does he live?"

"That's confidential information."

Gabe walked out of Theroux's office and stormed to the secretary's desk. He leaned forward with his hands flat on her desk. "I want the address—now."

She wrote it hastily down on a sticky note and handed it to him.

Gabe called Andre and gave him the address. "I need you to see if Zainer left the country or if he headed to California."

He tried to call his men on the ranch and couldn't get through. *Shit. I wanted Josephine to be in a blackout so she'd be protected for this. Our phones should work, though. Nothing.* He called Andre back and had him fly someone out pronto. They'd be there in an hour. He needed to get word to his men that the worst-case scenario might be on the ground and headed their way. He wanted to jump on the first plane there, also, but there was something he needed to do first.

Gabe walked back into Theroux's office. "You're calling a press conference."

"I am?"

"You are or I will make sure this story is spun in such a way that your company never recovers. You'll end up in jail right alongside Zainer. I've taken down mobsters and dirty politicians. You, my friend, are going to say exactly what I tell you to or have fun picking up the pieces of what's left when I'm done with your company."

His phone rang. "He's gone," Andre said. "I need time to track him down. I'll also put him on the FBI's radar."

"Do it," Gabe said, stepping off to the side so he couldn't be heard. "Theroux is going to make a statement to the press. I need to make sure Josephine is also legally safe when all of this ends."

Twenty minutes later Theroux stood in front of several cameras and microphones. He announced that evidence had been brought to his attention that cleared Roy Ashby of any wrongdoing. He added that the man responsible for his death was Felix Zainer and offered a reward for any information that led to his arrest. In a final statement, Theroux added that the final plans for the StealthOff, if they were recovered, would be donated to the US Army in Roy Ashby's name.

As soon as Theroux ended his announcement, Gabe rushed to the airport. His plane was fueled and ready. The flight back to the West Coast was the longest, most nerve-wracking trip he'd ever taken. Josephine needed him. *I told her I'd keep her safe.*

I can't lose her. I love her.

With her, I'm the man I should have always been.

Without her, who would I become?

Suddenly Gabe understood his father in a profound way that had eluded him until that moment.

Chapter Eighteen

JOSEPHINE CLOSED HER eyes for a moment and sought the peace of meditation. Fear wouldn't help her. Panic would make her sloppy. She needed to stay calm.

At noon, Dez knocked on the door of her lab and came in with a tray of food. "Where do you want it?" he asked with an easy smile.

"You can put it on the table near the monitor," she said, reaching for the Taser she'd made.

He set the tray down while saying, "I hope you don't mind, but I made a special dressing for you. It's Greek and my girlfriend's favorite."

Josephine walked up behind him quickly and pressed the Taser to him. He fell to the floor, shaking. She took the gun from his holster and stuck it in the back of her shorts then whipped out the duct tape and put it over his mouth. She tied his hands together then his feet. *I couldn't do any of this if you hadn't taught me how to defend myself, Dad. I now get why you believed working out daily was important, too.* Dragging him to the closet was a physical challenge. Dez loved food. She did it, though. Just as she placed him inside he started to struggle and scream behind the tape. She removed the radio from his ear then his phone from his breast pocket. "I'm sorry, Dez. You probably wouldn't have been the one to hurt me, but I couldn't take that chance. When I'm safe, I'll call someone and have all of you released." He shook his head and seemed to be adamant about something, but Josephine wasn't about to take the tape off his mouth. Maybe he doubted her. "I will. I promise. I'd never leave you like this." She closed the door of the closet and leaned her back against it.

One down.

The lights flickered in her lab and went out. She rushed over and turned on the battery-operated receiver. If it worked, their radios were now useless.

She waited. Once she left her lab, she could be shot by any of them. Here, in close quarters, she had the advantage. A light knock on the door was followed by Montee calling out, "Miss Ashby? Are you okay? Just wanted to check that you're not freaked out by the lights going off."

Josephine stood next to the door without answering him. He opened it, looked around, and was completely unprepared for the Tasing she gave him. He was on the floor before he even said a word. Josephine secured him with the duct tape, removed his gun, his radio and phone, and dragged him to the closet where Dez was. He was furious and kicking, but Josephine calmed him by threatening to Tase him again. She straightened and put a hand on her back. "You two should lay off the donuts for a while."

If a man could swear with his eyes, Montee was swearing at her. Josephine waved a finger at him. "This is your own fault. I liked all of you until I found out that you'd kill me if I tried to leave."

Both men shook their heads and tried to talk but it was all jumbled.

Josephine waved her finger at them again. "I heard the truth myself. I'm not leaving you to die, though. You're safe. And even if you don't deserve it, I'll send someone to let you out when I'm good and gone."

The waiting was the hardest part. An hour passed before she heard Julio and Kyle talking outside the door. "It's not like Montee to forget to check in. I haven't heard from Dez either."

"We'll make sure Josephine is secure, then I'll do a check of the area. They have to be somewhere."

They're together? Crap.

Josephine stood just inside the door. When they opened it she rushed to them. "Oh, thank God you're here. I thought I heard something outside."

Julio turned to look behind Kyle, and Josephine took the opportunity to zap Kyle. She gave Julio no time to react and Tasered him as well. Kyle started moving so she got him again and then Julio once more, just to be sure. *I'm pretty sure that can't kill them.*

She removed their guns and secured their arms and legs with the expertise of someone who was beginning to get good at it. She did duct tape their mouths, but she didn't bother with their radios because there was no one left for them to call. Nor did she bother to put them in the closet. They started flailing around and almost knocked a computer down on themselves. "Stop that. The only one who is going to hurt you is yourself. All I want to do is leave. Stay calm and you'll all be freed by whoever I can get to come here. I haven't thought that part through yet."

She tied back her hair, put on her helmet and began to push the bike out of the lab. She paused briefly and smiled with pride. "I didn't even need the zip ties."

The sound of car tires crunching on the gravel sent a shiver down her back. "Who is that?" she demanded of the two men in front of her.

They couldn't speak, but they shrugged.

She picked her Taser back up and began to push the bike farther out of the lab. If they didn't expect her to bolt, they might not be able to catch her. She stayed out of sight on the opposite side of the garage and watched for someone to exit the car. When the newcomer drew a gun and scanned the area, her stomach did a crazy flip. *Who is he? Does he know I'm here?*

I'm not faster than a bullet.

The snares. *All I have to do is lure him to where I'd put them in the grass along the side of the garage.* She threw a rock to catch his attention, waited for him to look away, then threw another. He headed toward the garage, and she prayed that the YouTube instructional videos she'd watched had actually produced a working snare.

The sound of a gun going off was followed by a long string of profanity. She peeked around the corner and saw the man hanging upside down with his gun on the ground just out of his reach. She picked it up turned it on the upside-down man.

"Who are you?" she demanded.

"Andre sent me."

"I don't know an Andre."

The guy looked nervous. He might have been lying. On the other hand, he was upside down with a gun pointed at him. *That might make him nervous, too.* "He works for Mr. Brannigan."

Gabe sent him. "What did he tell you to do?"

"He wants me to tell the guys that trouble might be on the way. They didn't give me the details, but Mr. Brannigan is on his way back from Connecticut and didn't think he could get here fast enough."

"Fast enough for what?"

"To stop whoever is coming." He gave her a sad look. "I'm here to protect you. Could you let me down? I'm getting nauseous."

"Who is coming? I don't understand." *Someone to take the bike? To take me?* "Who?"

"All I know is that Mr. Brannigan wanted the ranch to go dark so you wouldn't be involved in whatever went down. Andre said they were to keep you here and keep you safe at all costs. If anyone came for you they were to shoot to kill."

Josephine sat down, still facing the gun at the hanging man. "The order to shoot to kill was to *protect me?*"

"Yes."

She chewed her lip. *Did I get this all wrong?* "I want to believe you."

"Where is everyone? Why are you on your own?"

She made a face. "I could tell you, but you might be lying to me. If I let you down, suddenly I'm tied up in the lab instead of them."

"They're tied up in the lab?" The man's voice went up an octave.

She slapped her forehead. "I shouldn't have said that. I'm panicking. When I panic I get sloppy. I shouldn't tell you that, should I? Do you have any proof that you're not dangerous?"

The young man took his phone out of his front pocket. "You can call my mom. I told her where I was going."

"Your *mom?*"

He grimaced. "I just started working for Andre. I was only supposed to deliver a message."

GABE MADE IT to the ranch in record time. He jumped out of the car he'd had ready for him at the airport and scanned the area. Where were his men? Why hadn't he seen any of them on the way in? A car was parked mid-driveway, which he hoped belonged to the man Andre had sent.

Off to one side of the driveway movement caught his eye. It was Josephine getting onto her black stealth bike.

She rode up to him and pulled off her helmet. The move sent long waves of blonde hair cascading down her back. He took a step toward her, but she pulled a gun on him. *Déjà vu.*

"Stop right there."

He did, but he knew he had a big, stupid grin on his face. *She's alive. Thank God.* "Every time I think you can't get hotter, you find a way to."

She released the safety. "I want answers and I want them now. Where did you go?"

It was fun to play along. He raised both hands in a placating move. "You're upset now, but you will be so happy with me when I tell you."

"Stop evading the question and tell me."

"I went to Connecticut to clear your father's name and make sure you can safely come out of hiding without fear of being arrested or worse."

The gun shook in her hand, but it was still pointed at him. "How . . . how would you do that?"

He knew the next bit of news wouldn't be easy for her to hear. "I found the video of the night your father died."

She gasped and her hand went to her mouth. He knew watching the video wouldn't be easy for her, but it would give her the answers she sought. She needed that closure. "You're lying. It was gone."

"Money has a way of making things resurface."

"Show me the video."

He looked back at the car. "Shit. I don't have it on

my phone, and I didn't bring my laptop back with me. Andre has a copy of it. I'll see if he can send it." He tried to contact Andre but it went through to his voicemail. "He's not answering."

She waved the gun at him angrily. "If you went to Connecticut to help me, why would you keep it a secret? Why not tell me?"

"I didn't know what I'd find. You were safer off the grid."

She looked torn. "What was on the video?"

As he described it, she lowered the gun. By the time he finished she was crying. He stepped toward her, but she raised the gun again. She was in shock, cold and shaking. In a gentle tone he said, "You're safe now, Josie. The FBI is after Zainer. Raymean publicly declared your father's innocence. I hope you really meant that you didn't want to make money off the bike because I made sure the company also announced that the final design would be donated to the US Army. You're free. Zainer will be found and stopped and you have no more need to hide from anyone."

"How do I know you're not just telling me what I want to hear?" She looked about to cry again. It was heartbreaking, but he'd spend the rest of his life making her smile. First . . . first she needed the truth. He wished he could spare her the pain he knew she'd feel when she finally did watch the video, but she wouldn't endure it alone. He'd be right there for her—now and always.

"Before we get married we definitely need to work

out the trust issues we have. I went after the video because I believed you and your father were innocent. You need to believe me now."

"I heard you say I needed to be kept here. You gave your men an order to shoot to kill."

He smiled reassuringly. "To kill anyone who came to hurt you, yes. I gave that order. If someone came here from Raymean, they weren't going to leave alive."

"Why blackout the ranch?"

"I didn't want you to accidentally come out before I had cleared your name. Or have someone like Zainer find you before we had him on the run. The ranch blackout was the only way I thought I could insulate you until the danger was over."

"Bobby said the same thing earlier."

"Bobby?"

"Andre sent him. He just graduated from college. I don't think he should have a gun."

Gabe looked around. "Where is he? Where is everyone?"

Her instantly guilty expression was comical. It was quickly replaced, though, by the same direct look that had toppled him the first day they met. "They're all tied up in the lab."

He made a face as a thought occurred to him. "They're all still alive, right?"

"Of course they are. I'm not a murderer." The way she squared her shoulders and stood her ground could have inspired an army of men to follow her. *Will there ever be a day when she doesn't leave me near speechless?*

Gabe asked Josephine to give him a moment, and he headed over to the lab. He stood in front of his completely incapacitated, highly paid security team.

With scissors, he released Julio first then handed him the scissors and nodded for him to free the others. He leaned against the doorjamb, shaking his head, but didn't speak until all five men were back on their feet.

He pointed to the youngest man in the group. "I understand him, but what the hell happened to the rest of you? Dez, you're a Navy SEAL. Julio, you and Kyle have protected presidents. Do any of you see a problem with one woman being able to kick all your asses?"

Julio stepped forward and placed the scissors on the table. "With all due respect—"

"Respect is what I'm trying to have for you, but what would have happened if Zanier had been here?"

"He'd be dead," Dez said, with his shoulders proudly set back.

Gabe shook his head again in disgust.

Montee raised a hand in a silent call to halt the action. "You're looking at this the wrong way, boss."

"Really?"

Julio waved his hands in the air expressively. "We didn't hurt her."

Dez removed a last piece of duct tape off his arm. "Who would you rather have found in here? Us or her?"

The image of Josephine, tied up as they'd been, sent a protective surge of adrenaline through him. Had he come home and found her scared and restrained, he would have torn the men apart with his bare hands. He nodded abruptly. "Good call."

He left the men and returned to Josephine.

"You're amazing. I left four security men here with you and Andre sent an additional one. You thought they were going to hurt you so you locked them all up in your lab?"

"With a little help from Google and YouTube."

"You are the sexiest woman I've ever met. When I take you to meet my family, you should probably tone this down a bit, but don't for me." He took a good long look. "I love you just the way you are. In fact, you need to keep some of these outfits so we can role play with them. I've never been into that, but I think I want to be tied up. Although tying you up sounds great, too. We'll take turns."

"You want me to meet your family?" Her expression turned hopeful. The smile that crept across her face was one of the most beautiful he'd ever seen. She was magnificent. Fire. Sweet. Brilliant. *Mine.*

"As soon as my occupancy clause is over, I'll take you to meet all of them."

"I'd love that. You've told me so much about them." She looked down and then back up at him. "Do we have to tell them about all of this? I want a normal life. That won't be possible if I go public with everything."

"Normal?" He laughed then realized how serious she was. "I'll make you a deal: I'll tell everyone that we met on the ranch. That's it. Our boring version will be the one we take to the grave. No one needs to know the truth if—"

"If?" she parroted.

"You agree to marry me. I will never meet another woman who comes close to you. I think I fell in love with you the first time I saw your cute little ass hanging out of those jean shorts."

"That's not love," she said with a frown.

His first response was the big, stupid grin that talking to her always inspired. "Love can start there." When she didn't agree he arched an eyebrow in challenge. "You love me. What did it for you?"

She rolled her eyes. "First, you don't tell someone they love you. You wait until they say it."

He gave her what he hoped was a smoldering look. If she wanted him to woo her with poems and sweet words, he could do that, too, but he was also a man of action. "Are you saying you don't?"

She said nothing for a moment and merely met his gaze. His certainty wavered, then returned, then wavered again. A slow, wicked smile spread across her face. "Let me think about that for a moment." He frowned and she laughed. "Okay, okay, I do." She shot him a mischievous smile. "That first night under the stars when you were misnaming planets and looking so proud of yourself. It was so adorable I knew I was a goner."

"That wasn't exactly my best moment."

"And my ass hanging out of my shorts was mine?"

He raised and lowered a shoulder. "I guess it's a matter of perspective." He looked her over and his mood lightened. "So, will you?"

"What?"

"Marry me?"

"You're asking me right now?" She looked down at the gun she still had pointed at him. "Seriously?"

"We can tell everyone else I did it at a restaurant with flowers and everyone clapped, but really, is that what you'd want?"

"What kind of flowers?"

He threw back his head and laughed. "Josephine Ashby, you and I are going to have the most wonderful life together—as soon as you trust me. Ditch the gun."

She reset the safety and tossed it to one side. Gabe pulled her into his arms and kissed her soundly. When he finally raised his head he said, "You really did tie up all my men in the lab, didn't you?"

She nodded.

Gabe sent a text to Andre. Keeping Josephine safe trumped everything else. *Where is Zainer?*

He was just picked up trying to cross into Canada. We have him.

Good. All is secure here. Forward me the video. I'll call you later.

As soon as it downloaded, Gabe took her by the hand and led her to the bench on the porch of the house. If he could have taken her pain he would have. "It's not going to be easy to watch."

She took the phone. "I know."

They sat somberly beside each other while she watched the entire video. When it stopped, she played it again. When it ended for the second time, she went to play it again and Gabe took the phone out of her hands. "It's over."

She let out a soft sob as tears poured down her cheeks. "I knew it."

Gabe held her close. She was his new priority. More than anything he wanted to make sure the video brought her comfort and not more suffering. "He wanted to help that man. Your father was a good man until his very last breath."

She wiped tears away as they kept flowing down her cheeks. "He was. He was hardheaded, but in his heart he was a good person."

Gabe kissed her on the temple. "Like his daughter."

She nodded and sniffed.

Gabe continued, "I remember asking my father why he wanted us to live on a ranch. We could have all grown up in the city. He said places like this are where you find yourself. I never believed him, but I did find myself here. I understand now what my father wanted for me. It's not the house or canyon. It's how much of my parents live on here in the things they taught us and the memories I forgot we'd made here. I've always considered myself like my father, but until you, I didn't understand how my father could have changed so much after he lost our mother. I understand now. I can't imagine how empty my life would be without you in it."

Fresh tears poured down her cheeks, but she was smiling. "I feel the same way. I can't imagine you and all your ties not in my life." Josephine kissed his lips softly. "I will marry you, but I still want the pretty flowers and the ring."

"You'll get both if—"

"Another if?" she asked, this time with humor.

"If you stay here with me. I intend to keep the ranch, but I'm stuck here until the end of the occupancy clause. We could call it a honeymoon."

"Don't we have to be married first to have one of those?" She sniffed again and her smile widened.

"How about we call it practice for the real one?"

Chapter Nineteen

A MONTH LATER, dressed in a tux, Gabe paced the hallway in the main house of the ranch and hoped he'd made the right decision. *I should have invited my family.*

He'd spoken to his family about Josephine and how serious he was about her, but his relationship with them was a work in progress. He didn't want to tell Josephine they would be there if they weren't going to show up. He'd been absent from their lives long enough that he wouldn't have blamed them for skipping the event, but that morning when he'd set up the small white altar on the front lawn, he'd wished they were there. He not only wanted it for himself, but even if she wouldn't admit it, Josephine desperately wanted family.

I should have given that to her today.

A car pulled up in the driveway. Gabe walked out onto the porch and smiled. He walked down onto the driveway to meet his brother. "Luke."

"You look nervous. Ready for your big day?" Luke hugged him then went around the car to open the passenger doors. "Hope you don't mind that I brought company."

The woman had a warm, welcoming smile. "I'm Lizzie."

"I've heard a lot about you," Gabe said and leaned down to kiss her cheek. "I don't know how you knew to come, but I'm glad you did."

Lizzie introduced her niece, Kaitlyn, then said, "What was the name of the man who told us about today? Frank something?"

Luke nodded. "Frank Muller, the caretaker." He met Gabe's eyes intently. "Why didn't you tell me about today?"

Rather than go into the past, Gabe said, "It's been a rough year for everyone. We thought we'd make an announcement later."

"You're my brother, Gabe. This is where we all belong today—regardless of what else is going on in our lives. This is what matters."

Lizzy slid beneath his arm and hugged him. The way Luke gazed down at her was all Gabe needed to see to know that Luke would soon be following in his matrimonial footsteps.

With a smile, Luke said, "I'm not saying I wasn't surprised at the news. You're the last person I'd expect to leap without looking, but I guess it's about time you experienced a free fall. Now, maybe I can get you to go skydiving with me."

Gabe shook his head. "I haven't lost my mind; I've just fallen in love. And aren't your skydiving days behind

you? You have better ways to occupy your time now."
He'd nodded at Lizzie.

"I do feel less of a need to jump out of a plane to get
my heart pumping. I've got Lizzie for that." Luke's gaze
sought Lizzie's again.

Oh, yeah, he has it bad.

Another car pulled in. Hunter.

"Don't tell me, Frank Muller contacted you."

"Actually, it was Luke. He said you need a photogra-
pher today." After greeting everyone, he took out a
professional camera and snapped a photo of Gabe in his
tux and joked, "This will be part of my before and after
collage. Gabe when he still had his balls. Six months
from now when Josephine is picking out your ties and
you can't make a move without asking her permission, I
want to see if you're this happy."

The joke didn't stop Gabe from giving his brother a
back-slapping hug. "I've missed you, bro. Document all
you want. Life is only going to get better and better for
me. With her at my side there is no tree too high to
climb. She's the piece of me I didn't know I was
missing."

Hunter nodded in approval. "I can't imagine myself
ever settling down, but you look happy, Gabe. That's all
it takes for her to have my vote." Hunter took out his
phone and turned it toward Gabe. "Finn wanted to be
here but he couldn't get back in time. He has a serious
question for you, though."

"Gabe. I wanted to be there, but—"

"You are here," Gabe said. His heart swelled as he said the words. *More than anything else, this is what I wanted to give Josie. A family. I thought I'd have to chase them, pull them around to seeing things the way I do now. But here they are.* "Now, what's the question?"

With a heavy layer of little brother sarcasm, Finn asked, "When you start popping out kids and driving a mini-van, can I have your Aston Martin?"

"No," Gabe had answered with a straight face, and they all laughed.

A helicopter landed on the side lawn, announcing the arrival of James, Aunt Claire, and Knox. Gabe prepared himself for the hug he knew was coming and wasn't disappointed. She hugged him so tight he could barely breathe, but he didn't mind.

When she released him, she wagged a finger at him, but there was no anger in her eyes—just love. Her big hooped earrings shone in the sun, as bright as the sparkle in her eyes. "I'm so angry with you for not inviting me, but so happy that you're having your wedding here. And proud of you for keeping the ranch." She cupped his face with her hands. "Are you happy we're here?"

He took her hands in his and gave them each a light squeeze. "More than you know."

She blinked quickly. "Good, because I'm not leaving."

That inspired a general wave of laughter from the others.

Knox gave Gabe a clap on the shoulder. "None of us

are. Unless, of course, you don't feed us." He took out his phone. "I almost forgot. Max couldn't fly back in time, but he's standing by on his side."

Max waved from the phone. "Congratulations, bro. Glad you decided to keep the ranch. I'll come crash with you next time I'm in town. I hear your girl is shy. It's smart to marry her fast before we scare her off."

Not wanting to give too much away, Gabe said wryly, "She's not exactly a wilting flower. You'll like her."

"All that matters is that you do," Max said. "Happy for you, man."

Gabe was still smiling when James asked to speak to him on the side. Of all of his brothers, they were the most alike, and he could tell something was bothering James. "I know it's late in the game, but there's something you need to know before you get married today. I had Josephine investigated. She's not just a fill-in caretaker. Her father—"

Gabe hugged his brother spontaneously, an act that shocked James into silence. "Thank you for looking out for me. I mean that sincerely."

Still off kilter, James lowered his voice. "Her father was cleared of all wrong doing, but his death left many wondering about your fiancée. There's a rumor that her IQ is in the top one percent globally. Her father's work may have been hers. No one can pin down what she has been up to, but there is chatter that she went into hiding to work on something huge. That's why she was on the ranch."

"Where were you a month ago?" Gabe asked with irony that was lost on James.

"Right where I've always been. All you ever needed to do was pick up the phone."

I see that now. It took losing Dad and coming here to see that I am rich in ways that have nothing to do with my bank account. "I will from now on. But, James, keep what you learned about Josephine to yourself. It's nothing I didn't already know. She wants a normal life, and I want to give that to her."

James looked like he wanted to say more but nodded once.

Gabe wasn't an emotional man, however his gut twisted each time he imagined not having Josephine in his life. He wasn't afraid of marriage. He couldn't imagine a day without her in it. "I love her, James."

His words seemed to leave his brother unsettled, but Gabe understood why. Before Josephine, he'd thought he was happy. If asked, he would have said he had everything he wanted.

Then wham.

Love had a terrifying way of changing everything.

No man was ever ready, but every man was better for it.

ACROSS THE DRIVEWAY, Josephine was in her original bedroom in the guest house looking at herself in the mirror. She'd spent the morning trying to calm her nerves by playing music, soaking in the bath, and telling herself that being as happy as she was didn't mean anything was about to go wrong.

She applied a light layer of makeup then stepped into delicate layers of white satin and crystal roses. She was able to button most of the back herself, but when she came to a part she couldn't reach a wave of sadness hit her.

I wish you were here, Dad. Your big fingers would fumble with the buttons, but you'd make a joke that would have us both laughing about it.

She spun before the mirror. *I'm getting married. Can you believe it?* She smiled sadly. *You'd like Gabe. He's not like us, but that's good. I rev high and fast and he stays grounded. I need that. And he isn't intimidated by the real me. I can have the life I always dreamed of and still work on projects on the side.*

She tried again to reach the last few buttons again and couldn't. They'd have to wait until she saw either Gabe or one of his men. Still facing her reflection, she was temporarily succumbing to the void her father's death had left in her life. *I don't know what happens when we die. In nature, energy never disappears, it only changes form. Is that Heaven?*

Gabe makes me happy—happier than I ever imagined I could be, but that doesn't mean I don't still miss you every single day. I wish there were a way to know that you're okay. Sure you can't do a little tinkering up there and send me a sign that you're okay? Still with me?

A knock on the door surprised her and she jumped.

"Come in."

Frank Muller ducked his head shyly as he walked in. His normally unruly white hair had been trimmed and combed back. Despite his slight stature, he carried himself with dignity. "If you're ready, there's something I'd like to give you."

She looked over her shoulder at him and pointed at the six or seven undone buttons at the top. "Would you mind lending a hand first?"

He didn't meet her eyes, but Frank had always been shy like that. "Someone should invent something that would make that easier."

She smiled. "Someone did. It's called a zipper, but I fell in love with this dress."

He nodded, but his expression said he was still mulling possibilities. "There's no reason a zipper couldn't be automated."

Josephine chuckled. "No reason at all. You build it and I'll buy it." When he was directly behind her she held out her hand to him. "Thank you for coming back for the wedding."

He took her hand and gave it a tight squeeze. "You timed it right. My daughter and little Elynn are finally home. I'm not staying past tonight, but I wouldn't have missed this for anything."

Josephine's heart swelled with happiness for him. "You're a grandfather."

He gave her hand another squeeze then released it. "I am and it changes everything. My daughter said she needs me, so that's where I belong. I may even join a team somewhere. If someone steals my ideas, they steal them. What I won't let them rob from me is a moment with my granddaughter." He began to button the back of Josephine's dress. "Your father felt the same about you. You were his life."

Tears welled, but Josephine blinked them back. "He was not only my father, but also my best friend. It's hard to not have him here today."

After the last button was clasped, Frank said gently, "Come with me."

Josephine slipped on her white satin shoes and followed Frank into the living room. On the coffee table in front of the couch there were several thick leather albums. She looked at them and back to Frank for confirmation that it was okay to handle them.

"Go on," he said in a soft tone. "They're yours."

She sat gingerly on the edge of the couch and opened the top album. There was a photo of her as a baby along with a letter addressed to Frank. In the letter, her father told Frank all about how proud he was that she was already cutting teeth. Nothing written in the letter was of consequence, but the love her father had for her was evident in every line. She flipped through page after page. Through letters and photos to Frank her father had documented not only her life but how he had celebrated each of her achievements. The later leather journals listed her contributions to each of the projects they'd done together. There were photos of them together, photos of their inventions, and letters to accompany it all. She made a joke only because she was verging on bursting into tears. "You realize we're in a digital age."

Frank took a seat across from her. "I don't trust the Internet. Never have. Your father knew that. He also understood your decision to not be in the limelight, but that didn't make him less proud of you. I knew you'd be missing your daddy today and had these in the main house. I'm a man of science, so you won't hear me preaching, but a love like your father had for you doesn't disappear. He's here with you, Josephine, and he's happy his little girl found a man who could put up with her."

Josephine leaned forward and slapped his knee lightly. "Oh, you'll pay for that." Then she sat back and looked down at the journals again. "Thank you, Frank. For everything."

Frank nodded then said, "I saw some cars pull in. Did you change your mind about Gabe's family coming?"

Josephine had been too distracted to notice much of anything that morning. "They must be workers setting up the altar. We almost invited Gabe's family, but they're all very busy. We didn't want today to be focused on who couldn't be here, but instead simply about us choosing to spend the rest of our lives together."

"That doesn't seem right to me," Frank said with a sad shake of his head.

"We'll have a dinner with them later and announce that we're married. It's too much to ask them to drop what they're doing to be here."

"No expectations, no disappointment."

He knows me too well. "Something like that."

"Well, let's go then. Your future is waiting for you. Bet he's already there waiting for you."

Josephine was on her feet. "Am I late?"

With a cackle, Frank said, "How refreshing of you to worry. My daughter says she's never late, only highly anticipated. She also claims her daughter wasn't early, she was pre-released."

"You miss her already, don't you?"

A shadow darkened his eyes. "If I had a chance to go back, I would do so many things differently. I kept telling myself I had time to fix my relationship with my daughter. I'd do it next week, next month, right after I finished whatever project I was working on. Roy's death was a wake-up call for me. I'm comfortable here, but my daughter needs me and that's what matters the most."

She gave him a gentle smile. "Yes, it is."

"You remember that, Josephine. Your gift will take you many places, never let it be away from those you love."

She threw her arms around him. He accepted the hug awkwardly, but he was smiling. "You don't know what it means to have you here, Frank." She touched one of the leather journals. "I was missing my father, but I believe he's here today. There's no amount of scientific data that would convince me he's not. Does that sound odd?"

Frank walked to the door and opened it. "There are a great many things in life that cannot be explained or proven, but that doesn't make them less real. Love is one of them. The phenomenon of alien abductions is another."

Josephine's eyes flew to his, and she tried to gauge if he was joking or not.

He winked.

She laughed and he joined her. They linked arms and began to walk across the driveway together. They hadn't gotten far before she looked up and saw there was a small crowd gathered around Gabe. Their eyes met and he shrugged in apology.

Speaking to herself, and fighting back a mild panic, Josephine said thickly, "His family is here. Looks like he changed his mind."

"That's *your* family Josephine, if you let them be. Don't see them in terms of people who let you down. You go over there and love them with all your heart. And if they don't love you back, you come back to me. I'll build you a lab in my daughter's basement."

Josephine knew exactly what it had taken for Frank to put aside his paranoia and social fears and come here. He couldn't have chosen a better way to show how much he cared about her. "You have one very lucky daughter."

He blushed. "You tell her that next time she gets a thousand-dollar electric bill."

"I will," Josephine promised.

There wasn't time to say more. Gabe said something

to the people around him and they shuffled around into a half circle. He took his place beside the officiant and music began to play. Even the small number of onlookers added a level of formality to what had been a more casual ceremony. Josephine tightened her hand on Frank's arm. She wasn't sure if it was unfair to ask him then, but she did anyway. "Frank, will you walk me down the aisle?"

He raised his head proudly. "I'd be honored."

Chapter Twenty

TAKING DEEP, CALMING breaths as she went, Josephine walked with Frank across the lawn toward the little altar Gabe had put up beneath a flowered arbor. He left his spot with the officiant and strode toward her.

What is he doing? I'm supposed to walk to him. His family had all turned and were watching. She raised her chin and squared her shoulders.

Gabe stopped directly in front of her, and Frank stepped away. "You look gorgeous in anything you wear, but today—" He kissed her lips lightly. "Perfect."

Even as pleasure spread through her, she put her hand up to his chest in protest and sputtered against his lips. "*What* are you doing?"

He raised his head, his expression serious suddenly. "My family is here. I want to make sure that's okay with you."

Her worries about what they would think of the ceremony fell away. Gabe's love for her shone from his eyes. Very shortly she would be his wife. Everything else was frosting. She smiled brightly up at him. "I'm so glad you changed your mind and invited them."

"I didn't," he said and looked around until he spotted Frank a few feet away. "Thank you, Frank. I would have regretted not inviting them."

Frank ducked his head and stepped farther away, but he looked pleased.

Josephine almost ran after him to hug him again, but Gabe took her hand. There'd be enough time to thank Frank later. She met her soon-to-be husband's eyes. "That was a big deal for Frank. He doesn't reach out to anyone like that, but he doesn't want me to miss out on having a family."

"Nor do I," Gabe said and tucked her hand into the crook of his arm. "I want you to meet them."

"Now? Before the ceremony?"

She must have sounded concerned because he stopped and turned toward her again. "Coming back here opened my eyes to what I'd let fall to the wayside. You opened my eyes to the importance of family. My brothers will love you because I do. They may worry for me or tease you until you're tempted to use those kick boxing moves on them, but we'll make this work because this is what matters in the end. My father understood that. That's why he sent me here. He knew I was only half the man I was meant to be. I'm sure you and what you were doing here was the unexpected part of his plan, but I see beauty in the unexpected now. You gave me that."

They kissed and one of his brothers called out, "Not judging, but it seems like you have this backward."

Gabe laughed and she joined him. "Are you ready to not only meet my family, but join them?"

She winked and said, "Don't worry, if any of them acts up, I still have my duct tape. I'm going to play it sweet, though, so back me up."

He rested his forehead on hers. "They'll catch on eventually, but I love it. And I love you."

"I love you, too." She kissed him again. "So, are we doing this or what?"

He laughed again and raised his head. "Oh, yes."

Josephine normally would have analyzed the genetic similarities and differences between Gabe and his brothers, but that part of her brain had turned off for the day. She was riding on emotions and dreams.

Aunt Claire gave her a backbreaking tight hug. His brothers came over and welcomed her into the family one at a time. Knowing that one had brought the woman he loved with him warmed her heart. Lizzie might end up being her first sister-in-law. Josephine was going from no family to a huge one. She felt like she was floating. When she discovered that two of Gabe's brothers had heard too late to come but were joining them via video, it was the best wedding gift anyone could have ever given her. Or Gabe. He was all smiles.

James was the only brother who held back. He watched her closely and his welcome to the family wasn't as warm. Josephine saw the truth in his eyes; he knew her story. Even though she was in her wedding dress and the officiant kept looking across expectantly, Josephine whispered to Gabe, "Does James know?"

Gabe nodded. "He had you investigated. He doesn't know the whole story but he will later."

"Do you mind if I talk to him?"

Gabe looked across at James. "I can talk to him later."

"It'll just take a minute."

"I'll meet you at the altar," Gabe said with a final quick kiss.

Josephine chuckled. "That's how this is supposed to work."

Despite the eyebrows that flew up as she did it, Josephine asked James if she could talk to him on the side. He agreed and they stepped away from the rest of the family.

Josephine jumped right in. "I love Gabe. Whatever you think you know or don't know, that's what matters."

His expression tightened. "It wasn't my intention to offend you. My brother is important to me. If you're not who you appear to be, be careful. You mess with him, you mess with all of us."

Frank's words came to her. *Love them with all your heart.* She leaned toward him and said confidentially, "I'm not who I appear to be at all, but that's part of what your brother loves about me. I'm not offended. Actually, I would have been disappointed in you if you weren't worried for your brother. I know you don't trust me yet, but I'll have the next sixty or so years to win you over. I'm not worried."

James looked from her to Gabe and back. "He doesn't look worried at all that we're talking."

"Because he knows me. He knows I'd never do anything to hurt him or his family—my family if you accept me into yours."

James studied her face for a moment then smiled. "I look like a jackass right now, don't I?"

She linked her arm in his. "No, you look like the kind of protective older brother I always wanted. Now, if you don't mind, I'm ready to get this party started."

They walked back to where Gabe was standing. As they passed Frank he smiled in approval. James handed her off to Gabe and the two brothers shared a look.

The officiant cleared his throat. Gabe and Josephine turned toward each other in front of him, but Gabe leaned forward and said, "He likes you."

"He *loves* you," Josephine whispered back. "So, he already has a place in my heart."

Neither of them was paying attention as the officiant started the ceremony. They were too busy smiling at each other.

"Wait," a male voice called out, temporarily calling the ceremony to a halt. Montee approached the altar from the side. One of his hands was behind his back. "I do know a reason they can't marry yet."

A silence hung heavily in the air. Josephine turned to face him.

Montee's face transformed with a huge smile. "She doesn't have her bouquet yet." He handed her a bunch of lilies.

With all that had gone on leading up to the wedding, Josephine had completely forgotten to order a bouquet. She accepted it with a teary, grateful smile. When her hand closed around it, though, she burst out laughing. The stems of the flowers were wrapped in duct tape. She showed it to Gabe who also burst out laughing before shaking Montee's hand.

"Are we ready?" the officiant asked.

Gabe pulled Josephine into his arms. "Are we? Ready? I know I am."

"Bring on forever. I'm all in," she answered, and they kissed again.

One of her brothers said, "They've got this all wrong."

Aunt Claire's voice sang out, "No, it looks like they've got it just right."

THE END

Want to read more from this series? Continue on with Hunter by NYT's Bestselling Author, Melody Anne.

Blurb

When Hunter Brannigan loses his father and is sent a map, he doesn't know what to think. Is it a joke? Was the old man going senile at the end? The attorney sending the map assures him the piece of paper was definitely from his father and he must follow the clues to find himself.

Hunter has been running from anything even remotely resembling responsibility for a very long time. He's a world renowned Photo Journalist, traveling the seven continents in pursuit of the next great shot. He's been in the heart of the trauma during war time, natural disasters, and life-altering moments, always on the other side of the lens, never getting emotionally involved. His father's last wish for him is to put himself within the pictures he's famous for.

Deciding to humor his father's last request, he stumbles upon Rebekah Kingsley III, an uptight History Professor who desperately needs to let her hair down. Though he has his doubts she can get dirty long enough to help him, something about her won't let him walk so easily this time. Will she be enough to make him settle down, or will he leave her with nothing but a picture of what could have been.

Dear Readers,

I was over the moon when I was asked to participate in this series. I still get goosebumps when I see my book next to those of many of favorite authors: Barbara Freethy, Melody Anne, Christie Ridgway, Lynn Raye Harris, Roxanne St. Claire and JoAnn Ross. Seven full-length love stories about seven sexy men and the women who tame them.

If you're new to my books,
I write fun, spicy bathtub reads about sexy billionaires and hot cowboys.

Want to meet your next addiction?

Start with a FREE download of Maid for the Billionaire.

ruthcardello.com/maid-for-the-billionaire

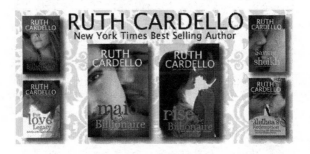

Dominic Corisi is one alpha hero who will steal your heart.

His story continues with the Andrade family.

You'll visit old friends and make new ones in the Barrington Billionaire Series.

Love when different authors write in the same world? Check out my Barrington Billionaire Synchronized Series.

ruthcardello.com/the-barrington-billionaires

Three authors, three series, all in the same world with character crossover into each.

About the Author

Ruth Cardello was born the youngest of 11 children in a small city in southern Massachusetts. She spent her young adult years moving as far away as she could from her large extended family. She lived in Boston, Paris, Orlando, New York—then came full circle and moved back to New England. She now happily lives one town over from the one she was born in. For her, family trumped the warmer weather and international scene.

She was an educator for 20 years, the last 11 as a kindergarten teacher. When her school district began cutting jobs, Ruth turned a serious eye toward her second love– writing and has never been happier. When she's not writing, you can find her chasing her children around her small farm, riding her horses, or connecting with her readers online.

Contact Ruth:

Website: RuthCardello.com
Email: Minouri@aol.com
FaceBook: Author Ruth Cardello
Twitter: @RuthieCardello

56805256R00146

Made in the USA
Lexington, KY
30 October 2016